The pREZident

Published by

Pow Wow Communications, LLC

4772 Haxton Way

Ferndale, WA 98248

Tim,

It was great to work along

Book Concept by Aaron Thomas.

Eide you, Keep up the great work. Enjoy.

1

This book is dedicated to those who possess positive energy and see things as a 'glass half full' for life presents us with things that in the end we need to laugh, love and pray about.

"The pREZident"

and to all tribal People

for you have so much resilience

and deserve the Earth and all that

it has to offer.

Prayers to former tribal leaders who have passed on: Billy Frank Jr., Earl Thomas Sr., Willie Jones Sr., Sam Cagey and current leaders: Brian Cladoosby, Ernie Stevens Jr. and the silent masses of leaders in Indian Country.

For without your hard work and dedication, we wouldn't be as successful as we are today.

Chapter 1: The Dream Team

"Welcome to tonight's Libertarian Forum, here on Fusion TV. Tonight, we'll hear from Presidential Candidates, John Dungberry and Barry Whiteman," said Katie Stevenson, host of the Libertarian Forum.

"Let's start with Governor Dungberry, who for all intents and purposes should be the Republican nominee for President. As you can see in this video clip, Dungberry and now-current Republican nominee Sherry Montgomery had a ...well, let's call it a .. "disagreement" during the Republican candidate's debate back in May," Stevenson said.

The TV clip shows the two candidates on a stage at the University of Houston. Each candidate is standing behind their podium where the hot white lights beam down exposing their every expression.

Sherry is wearing a beautiful suit with a red bow tie, white button up, navy blue coat and skirt that goes all the way to her ankles.

Her wardrobe, her verbal language and non-verbal language is all on cue, exactly what her handlers told her to say and do.

Dungberry has continued his strategy of doing exactly the opposite of Sherry's campaign. He is gaining popularity for being 'the electable candidate' and winning both Republican and Democrat voters as the months leading up to the Presidential election continues.

On stage, he is wearing his normal outlandish suits, as he is known for 'peacocking' or sticking out from the crowd. This suit he's wearing this night is literally red, white and blue. The only thing he's missing from looking like 'Uncle Sam' is the long white beard and red, white and blue top hat.

"Governor DUNG-berry," Montgomery said during the candidate's debate, slowly raising her hand and pointing her finger at him. "Didn't you approve, under YOUR administration, to allow several CONVICTED felons to walk free early this year."

Dungberry grips the podium and looks down. He takes a deep breath and looks back over to Montgomery.

"Now, if I'm not mistaken, these CONVICTED felons were from your home state of Ohio and even more absurd, they happen to be from the same neighborhood you grew up in...in...in..Cleveland of all places...who grows up in Cleveland anyway, ...that city is the armpit of America, the funny farm that only grows LOSERS anyway....but I digress..," Sherry said.

"Getting back to these CONVICTED FELONS, why did you allow them to just simply walk away, scot-free, knowing that these felons committed these heinous crimes?" Montgomery asked.

"Now, first of all, Miss Sherry, Cleveland, ...my city, that I hail from isn't what you say it is," Dungberry said in a strong southern draw, looking straight into the camera, smiling. Montgomery rolls her eyes in disgust.

"Secondly, the citizens that were in jail were convicted, you are correct in sayin' that. However, their attorney did a great job of showin' new evidence that proved that they had nuttin' to do wit' the kitten fights, that our administration has gone in and eradicated off the wonderful streets of Cleveland, Ohio."

"New evidence?" Montgomery interrupted Dungberry, who had already had enough of his female counterpart. Leading up to the debate, her team had created a campaign making fun of his last name, making fun of Cleveland, mocking his southern draw (which in honesty, how does a man from Cleveland, Ohio have a southern draw? He never once lived in Texas or any southern state?).

"When these CONVICTED felons got out, guess what was the first thing they decided to do Governor? Yup, that's right, they went back into your dumpy streets of Cleveland and they began to start a bar fight at what is the name of that crappy dive bar again?... (snapping her fingers)...oh, that's right, it's called "The Crappy Dive Bar of Cleveland!" she pounds her hand on the podium.

Dungberry is looking down, his face is getting red and he begins to sweat. It is taking every little bit of energy not to go over to her smug face and punch her right between her beady little eyes. He takes a deep breath.

"The four men you're bringin' up are model citizens of the beautiful city of Cleveland. They are volunteers in the local shelter for battered women, they coach little league and so what if they happen to live together and are pretty much married to each other, I support the Gay and Lesbian community," Dungberry said.

As each word he utters, Montgomery is silently rolling her eyes, mocking his words with her mouth and the crowd is slowly buying into her immature shenanigans.

Dungberry tries to continue but he notices the audience is beginning to laugh.

"You have no idea how to run a successful gov'ment and the more I stand up here…" he notices more and more laughing and he looks over at Montgomery who is almost dancing, shrugging her shoulders with every word that comes out of Dungberry's thin lips.

"…I, I,…." Dungberry tosses his podium to the side and dives at Montgomery. His 6'3" skinny frame, outlandish suit goes flying in the air and he successfully tackles the small, 5'4" Montgomery. The audience shutters as they cannot believe what they just witnessed.

Within a millisecond of Dungberry on top of Montgomery, (flashes of bulbs are now blanketing the entire stage as photographers are all enjoying every tasty bite that is happening on stage) secret service agents come storming out of the sides of the stage and pull the two people off of each other.

Montgomery gets helped up from her secret service agents and Dungberry does too. Montgomery's hair is all frazzled, Dungberry fixes his bow tie.

The TV footage comes back to a live shot with Katie Stevenson at the Libertarian Candidates Forum.

"So, Dungberry gets bucked off the Republican ticket because Republican voters said they cannot fathom voting for someone who hurts women," Stevenson, the emcee for the candidate's forum said, as the TV show flashes back to her on the main stage.

"We know Dungberry hails from the eh' hem, great city of Cleveland, he's the Ohio State Governor, the father of three kids and a husband to Mary Dungberry for over 30 years. But who is his running mate?

6

"He is no other than Barry Whiteman, a Native American who has been the President of the National Congress of American Indians for the past 6 years. Whiteman, and no he is not even white, ..more about that in a minute, is a Tulalip Tribes tribal member which is a reservation just north of the Emerald City or Seattle.

"Whiteman is not married, he's never been a governor, heck he's never even been on city or county council. He represents a State that isn't known for its political savvy and doesn't carry a lot of weight for electoral votes; so why him?

"Let's go to a clip of an interview we had with Dungberry earlier this morning.."

There is a single video shot of Dungberry in a chair as he is getting his TV makeup on. He's got the thin paper that covers up his collar so to ensure that the makeup artist doesn't get foundation on his shirt.

"Why Barry Whiteman as my running mate?" Dungberry rhetorically asks. "I'll tell you why I chose him as my running mate. (long pause)...you can't duplicate another Barry Whiteman. Barry represents what's good in America.

"He is a good-hearted, smart, decent man who has lead his Native race of people through good and not-so-good times," he said in the southern draw and with a huge grin on his face.

"So, it's not because he was the only one who said yes to running with you on the Libertarian ticket?" said the reporter who was off-camera.

"Absolutely not, shame on you for saying such a thing," Dungberry said smiling. "What source did you get that ludicrous information from?"

"Your wife, Mrs. Dungberry," the reporter said.

Dungberry makes the 'cut' sign and pushes the camera away from his face.

"Okay, well he says he didn't choose Whiteman because there wasn't anyone else who would run with him, but that remains to be seen," said Stevenson. "What else remains to be seen as how these two running mates that Dungberry's campaign calls 'The Dream Team,' will fare in today's Libertarian candidate's forum."

"Let's check in on Barry Whiteman, Libertarian Vice President hopeful," Stevenson said. The camera moves into the green room where Whiteman is at. In the distance, as the camera is moving into the room, the viewers could see a man running left and right. The camera goes in closer and its Whiteman playing Pokemon Go.

"Excuse me! Excuse me!" Whiteman says as he darts passed people who are actually doing work trying to get what they need done before the two candidates go up on stage.

Whiteman bumps into the camera man, which makes the video shot also jerk to the left and then back to the right, focusing on Whiteman.

"YES!! I got them all! Oh, sorry about that, I like to Pokey-Go as I get ready for a big moment. You know before big meetings, before any interview..." Whiteman says as he wipes his sweat off his forehead and uses the same hand to shake the reporter's hand.

"Oh, sorry about that," Whiteman says referring to the sweat that he just transferred to the reporter.

Off camera, the reporter asks: "Who is Barry Whiteman?"

"I'm part of the Dream Team baby! Whoo hoo! I like to call us the Double Berries...we're both sweet, good and healthy for you," Whiteman says as he winks into the camera.

A chair gets pulled up to the back of Whiteman and the makeup artist asks him to have a seat on it. He obliges and continues the interview as they start to dab foundation on his dark forehead. A thin piece of paper also gets stuffed into his collar to protect it from the makeup.

The reporter says: "So, you come from Native America, our Nation's First People. Is this a moral victory for Indian Country to have a tribal person running for one of the biggest jobs in the world?"

"Moral victory? Shoot, this would make everyone cream their pants," Whiteman says chuckling hard. "Hell, the BIA, the right-wing Nazis ,...all I know is that the Europeans and the Japs would absolutely love the fact that a Native would be working in the White House."

"Isn't saying Japs a not-so-political thing to say, Mr. Whiteman?" the reporter asks.

"Saying Japs is nothing compared to what the candidates in the other political parties have said about us and about me specifically," Whiteman said.

"What did they say specifically?" Barry was asked.

"You can't go around saying that all Natives are this or that all Natives are that. It would be like me saying that all white people are racist, which my auntie mom back on the Tulalip rez really truly believes....hi Auntie Z!" Whiteman exclaims into the camera.

"Well, that was Vice President hopeful Barry Whiteman who calls he and Dungberry, the double berries," Stevenson said. "Double berries...the Dream Team? We'll see now won't we?"

Off camera, Dungberry is on his cell phone talking to one of his handlers who needed to go out and get a lucky white rabbit's foot. One of the interns forgot to go get it and Dungberry swears that it works.

"Alright, alright, I understand what you're sayin'," Dungberry says as he walks into Whiteman's green room. "Where's that Injun?"

"Ah, I think he's in the closet sir," said one of Dungberry's assistants.

"Closet?" Dungberry asks.

The assistant points over to the closet to the right of where they were standing. Dungberry opens the door and Whiteman is in there, lights off, sitting on the floor, praying.

The sudden door opening frightens Whiteman and he turns around: "Oh, hi there partner. How may I help you?"

"What you doin' man?" Dungberry asks, rolling his eyes talking down to him.

"Oh, you know, I'm just taking a minute to find my center, you ever do that?" Whiteman said.

"Yeah, I call it my Ohio two-step," Dungberry replied. Whiteman looked a bit confused.

"I eat, then I take a crap! Now get up and let's go win this election!" Dungberry said as he turned around and walked out of Whiteman's green room with his small entourage following him.

A Fusion TV Producer is standing on the side of the two candidates. "We'll be on camera in 10 seconds!!"

Stevenson is gathering her notes and a makeup artist comes and dabs another coat of powder over her t-zone and she dashes on stage.

 "Welcome back! I'm here with Presidential hopefuls John Dungberry and Barry Whiteman, thank you gentlemen for taking some time to talk to the voting public.

"Let's talk foreign policy and I'll address this question to you Governor Dungberry, since you are the only one that has any real experience with foreign policy."

"Now hold your fussy little britches young lady," Dungberry interrupted her. "That's just not true. My runnin' mate and friend Barry Whiteman has been dealing with foreign policy his entire life.

"Sure, I mean, look at him. He's a tribal member from the great Tulalip Tribes. Their people have done dealt with the United States for over 130 years, it don't get much foreign than that!"

A round of applause echoes through the auditorium.

"Now I don't pretend to say these things just to get a pat on the back," Dungberry said. "I say them because we have done real injustice to Native Americans throughout the years and we owe them our debt of thanks for takin' our ancestors, the pilgrims, into their homes, showin' us how to hunt, or how to gather. Hell if it weren't for them, we would all be dead today!"

Another round of applause echoes through the auditorium.

"Alright, then I'll ask the question to Mr. Whiteman," Stevenson turns her attention to Whiteman who is sitting next to Dungberry, wearing a Tulalip Tribes bolo tie, tan corduroy jacket and dark blue jeans with some dark brown cowboy boots.

"Let's talk about Yemen," Stevenson said, moving in her seat to get more comfortable. "The United States has sold millions of dollars-worth of weapons to Saudi Arabia and because of this, there have been new terrorists groups popping up.

"If you two are elected President and Vice President, will you stand up to the Saudi monarchy to try and put an end to the wars that we, essentially helped create?" Stevenson asked.

"Let me start out by saying, thank you or 'hyshqe' for having the two of us here and thank the Akokisa Tribe for allowing us to have this event here on their homelands.

"I compare what I've seen in Saudi Arabia to that of our tribal nations' policies. You see, we, just as President Obama and President Bush before him, all do the best we can. We call it 'estitem-sen' or 'I'm doing the best I can'.

"Are we perfect people? No one on this earth is perfect. Was selling guns and bombs to Saudi Arabia the best thing for us? Probably not; as Indian people, we do the best we can to create policies that will help not only this generation but also the next generation of people.

"We make hard, educated decisions; but moreover, we go talk to our community members. We ask them for their input and for as long as I've been watching how all of the administrations have been conducting business; I have yet to see one that did it that way.

"An administration under the double berries or the Dream Team, will do just that. We will go out and ask our constituents what they think about decisions like our foreign policies and our policies here at home."

A round of applause interrupts him.

"Won't that take too long Mr. Whiteman?" Stevenson asked.

"Probably..probably..but think about it. If we fail to ask our People what they think about the decisions we make, then what's this all for? Why did they even take the time to vote for us?"

The decibel levels of the applause in the audience starts to escalate with every word Whiteman says.

"For if we don't really.., truly, act on behalf of the people of the United States, then we're just paid puppets, acting on behalf of the simple minority and not on behalf of those who make this country what we are; the middle class, the lower class of people who make up 99% of the great United States of America!"

The entire auditorium erupts with cheers, they stand on their feet and it takes several attempts by Stevenson to calm them down.

The forum continued for the next 60 minutes with Stevenson asking the two candidates several questions ranging from education, to terrorism both at home and abroad.

The two men stood up, hugged and walked out to the center of the stage, waving their hand up in the air and thanking each of the persons that were in attendance.

The next morning, pandemonium strikes the political world; has The Dream Team done enough to make this a three-race election campaign?

Chapter 2: Knock Yourselves Out

It was mid-August and the tribal leaders decided to hold a special forum to discuss the effects of having a member of a tribe on a Presidential ticket.

Some tribal leaders were happy that there was an option for them to endorse, an option that they felt good in giving their time, their funding and their opinion to their constituents.

"I for one am happy that we have on the Presidential ticket a person that has seen what we've seen, been through what we've been through," said Darnell Stevens, Swinomish tribal chairman.

"I don't know who the hell Barry Whiteman is?" rhetorically asked by Margerie Upola, Chairperson of the Agua Caliente tribe in California. "What the hell is up with his last name? WHITE-man??"

The audience attending the National Congress of American Indians (NCAI) was made up of mostly tribal leaders, elders and team members of the tribal leaders. They all busted out laughing when they heard chairperson Upola's comment.

"Order,....order.., we need to stay focused and give each other the respect we deserve!" exclaimed Eunice Washington, NCAI's President and Chairperson of the Bois Forte Band of Chippewa in Minnesota.

"At the forefront of what we have here is the opportunity to be able to know and understand who Barry Whiteman is, however, if elected, he'd only be the Vice President.

"We really need to know and understand who John Dungberry is," Washington said. "Yes, I know we've had several sessions, loooong sessions about Montgomery and Duckson, but since Dungberry named Whiteman his running mate, we need to do our due diligence with Dungberry.

"Now, has anyone in the greater Ohio area ever worked with Governor Dungberry?" Washington asked.

Several hands shot up and one-by-one, they explained how Dungberry's communication and professionalism helped them get through several key moments for their tribes.

On the contrary, they also mentioned his hot temper and how he does let the small stuff seem to get under his skin.

By the end of that session, they were able to agree to endorse the Dungberry/Whiteman ticket, which was big for Dungberry because it gave them more notoriety in the election circles and more importantly, gave them a ton more funding for their campaign.

All of the tribal chairs came home from the special session and throughout their own processes, they helped get-out-the-vote (GOTV), by educating their own tribal members and helping them register for the election and ultimately voting for Dungberry and Whiteman.

"Welcome to The Situation Room, my name is Janice Thompson in for Wolfe Blitzer. Breaking news this evening shows Republican Presidential nominee Sheri Montgomery/Alfred Davis leading Democratic Presidential Nominee Donald Duckson/Boyd Rubio by a slim 5 percentage points in the latest Gallup survey.

"Their lead has dropped to 5 percent, down from 12 percent just a month ago. Now, what is interesting is that although

Montgomery's lead has dropped, Duckson's support has only increased by 1 point.

"So, who picked up the six-point differential? Enter Libertarian Presidential nominees John Dungberry and Barry Whiteman.

"We'll now bring in political director for CNN, Theodore Yost; Theo, what has been the secret sauce for this sudden change with only 3 months left before the general election?"

"Well Janice, the secret formula for the self-proclaimed "Dream Team" has been pretty simple. Let Montgomery and Duckson duke it out and watch them knock themselves out," Yost said.

Meanwhile, Sherry Montgomery is in her office reviewing her statements that she'll give in a Fox News interview in about 20 minutes.

"Can you believe this!!" exclaimed Montgomery's campaign manager David Gump.

Donald Duckson is sitting at home, awaiting his wife to get ready for a campaign fundraiser they are about to go to.

"This is bullshit!" yelled Duckson's campaign manager Worley Peterson, at the campaign office as he sees the breaking news on TV.

Both Republican and Democratic campaigns were in shock. Never in the history of elections has any party other than a republican or a democrat ever won the presidential election.

Although the decline in support for Montgomery was less than 10 points, statisticians all around the world took note in the latest Gallup poll because it wasn't the amount of points that changed, but the fact that there was such an abrupt change in trend.

"I liken shift in support to a thunderstorm in the middle of a sunny day," said Sam Oliver, statistician at Washington State University who was quoted in a New York Times article.

"Voters are clearly beginning to like the message that the Libertarians are saying, but I have to say it, I don't think it's their message or strategy that is winning support," Yost said.

"Let's take a look at what has happened in the recent weeks leading up to the Gallup poll," Yost said as the TV show flips the tape on to show Montgomery speaking at a rally 30 days ago:

Sherry Montgomery is standing behind a podium that has a 20"x20" sign on it that says 'The Future is Now'. She is speaking into the microphone. "Donald Duck-son cannot lead this country; he's too unfit to lead the United States. I understand he is 170 lbs and just ran the Boston Marathon, but he is still unfit!" Montgomery said to the thousands that were in attendance.

The TV camera comes back to Yost: "On the Democratic side, let's hear what Donald Duckson said at his support rally 30 days ago."

Duckson is standing behind a podium and in front of a large group of people who are of different ethnicities. His podium has a 25"x20" sign that reads, 'On With the Show!' a campaign message that is a bit difficult to explain. "If you vote for Montgomery, there is clearly something wrong with you. She has a drinking problem, she swears all the time and if you vote for her, you are just like her, a loser!"

Montgomery: "We've been at this campaign for what feels like an eternity. I've gone to so many homes and there isn't one good thing that any of the voters I've talked to has ever said about Donald Duck."

Duckson: "Yeah, she drinks…a LOT! I mean, she can drink you under the table (pointing at members of the audience sitting in the front row), and you and you and you!"

Montgomery: "How he got through grade school is beyond me. I mean look at how he dresses, my 10-year-old son has a better wardrobe that him!"

Duckson: "Why do you think her name is Sherry? Al-COOOO-Holic!!"

Montgomery: "He's a cartoon. Yeah, just like his name says..Donald Duck..you might as well call him that from now on…"

A panel on CNN is now on TV, talking about the health of both campaigns and how they have strategized thus far with only 82 days left until "Super Tuesday".

CNN commentator Angela Rye is the host, talking to David Satler, former advisor to Republican Senator John McCain and James Blufield, former advisor to Democrat Senator John Kerry.

"With less than 90 days to go, gentlemen, how would you rate the two campaigns thus far?" Rye asked.

"I'd give both of them a solid -4 on the Richter scale," Blufield said. "This is a whole new definition of politics, one that I would phrase is less than 'gutter' politics, but more like septic tank or worse off, … 'Sewer Politics' is what we're seeing from both camps!"

"David, do you agree?" Rye asked.

"Absolutely! I mean, who the hell advised these two candidates as James says, 'play in the sewer'? I would be ashamed of myself if I played any role in how these two are going about it."

Rye said: "The voting public is agreeing with the both of you, as the latest Gallup Poll points to a drop in the lead for not only Montgomery but also a drop in points to the Dungberry campaign too.

"As you can see in the graph, with 125 days until the election, both camps were in a steady trend, having more than 90% of the total being divided by Montgomery at 52% and Duckson at 48%.

"Now with 82 days, the divide is now split three ways, with Montgomery dropping down to 42%, Duckson at 32% and now Dungberry at 24%!"

Both guests on the show are visibly shocked and even one of the two responded with an expletive which producers of the show had to unexpectedly bleep out of the 10-second delay.

"How has Dungberry and Whiteman snuck into this race?" Rye asked.

"It's pretty simple Angela. Dungberry's camp is staying out of the sewer!" Blufield said smiling.

"Yeah, I echo what he just said, I mean, the Dungberry team is just hitting their marks on what they *can do* for the country and not what the other ones *cannot* do or *have not* done," Satler said.

"So, just staying the course?" Rye said.

"Yup, pretty much; it's been a really refreshing campaign I have to admit!" Satler replied.

"Refreshing how?" Rye asked. "Their message was the same one that Barack Obama used during the last eight years."

"It's refreshing because it so much more different than the ones that Duckson and Montgomery are using. Different in this case, is good..very good," Blufield said.

It is now 40 days until Election Day and both Republican and Democrat camps are really nervous about their future. A turn of events would soon rock this election and make traditional pundits of elections scratch their heads in wonderment.

"Hot damn, look at those numbers Marcus!" Dungberry said to his right hand man, Marcus Peterson, handing him the latest poll numbers.

"I know sir, I cannot believe it!" Peterson said.

"Can't believe it? Why not?" Dungberry asked.

"I mean.. I mean.." Marcus stammered.

"You better start believin', heck, in fact let's begin usin' that as our campaign war cry!" Dungberry instructed. "Yeah, I can see it now Marcus; Vote Dungberry, A President You Can Believe In".

Marcus had his notepad out and was jotting down the new campaign slogan. He began to walk away when Dungberry stopped him.

"Oh Marcus ol' boy? I also want just the letter 'B' on some half-dollar sized pin buttons," Dungberry ordered.

"The letter 'B' sir?" Marcus asked.

Dungberry put his foot up on a small chair that was sitting next to a large window overlooking Cleveland's downtown area. He looked outside and raised his hands to gesture.

"Yup, 'B' stands for BELIEVE...yup, gosh darn it (clapped his hands one time), we'll focus on that word, BELIEVE!" Dungberry excitedly said.

"I believe sir!" Marcus responded.

"Atta boy! That's right, believe!!" Dungberry said as he straightened up his pants near his waist and tucked in his button up shirt a bit more.

Journalists, voters and media pundits all called for a three-person debate, the first-of-its-kind. All three candidates agreed and the first debate was held at New York University, with Lester Holt from NBC News moderating the first debate.

The clear goal for Duckson and Sherry Montgomery was to make Dungberry the least liked, least credible person up on that stage to garner the support back that Dungberry took from them over the past 40 days.

The tactic to make Dungberry out to be a fool, backfired, because there was too much animosity between Duckson and Montgomery. They spent 80% of their time calling each other out and most people would agree that Dungberry was the clear winner of debate #1.

People would also agree that Holt was not a very good moderator, as he allowed Duckson and Montgomery way too much flexibility with their time on the microphone.

Holt would be replaced by two people for debate #2 as CNN's Anderson Cooper and ABC's Martha Raddatz would moderate that one.

The strategy going into this one for Duckson and Montgomery was to again try and attack Dungberry, but instead, they were the ones that were being attacked as Dungberry hit them time and time again about what they didn't do while they were in office.

It is now 30-days until election day and Dungberry's campaign had moved into a three-way tie for voter popularity: 32%-32%-32% with an error margin of about +/- 3%.

Dungberry's 'Believe' message began to really resonate with voters and with only 10 days left until "Super Tuesday", his poll numbers outweighed Montgomery and Duckson's popularity.

The third and final debate was moderated by Fox News' anchor, Chris Wallace who by many people going into the debate, would think he would slant his questions to support Montgomery, the Republican candidate.

Unfortunately for her, most Republicans were now jumping ship and moving their support for Dungberry because a rumor had been leaked just before the third debate that Montgomery had a tape that incriminated her of using racial slurs while she was drinking at a fundraiser back in May.

Dungberry and Duckson both laid haymakers to Montgomery's reputation throughout the 90-minute debate.

Dungberry was now in the lead with him garnering 42% and Montgomery and Duckson each with 28%.

All the late night TV hosts were having a field day at the expense of Montgomery and Duckson:

Jimmy Fallon: "The only thing that is stopping a non-Republican and non-Democrat from winning the White House is a UFO and even that is more likely to happen than Montgomery or Duckson winning!"

Jimmy Kimmel: "Oh, it's great that we're making history, oh..and under the word 'history' in the dictionary you see Montgomery and Duckson's picture with them waving 'goodbye'..'nice to know ya,' 'ta ta.'

Stephen Colbert: "Montgomery and Duckson, you had one job! Don't get fired!!"

Seth Meyers: "Whatever Dungberry is drinking, I want some. Kool-aid, Gator-Aid, gasoline..hell, I'll drink his urine because that is what winning tastes like! Hash-tag WINNING URINE!"

It is Tuesday, November 8th, 2016 and all eyes are on the Dungberry/Whiteman campaign train or in short, it is their election to lose.

"Welcome to Election Night!" Wolfe Blitzer announces into the TV camera in the CNN studios. "My name is Wolfe Blitzer and by all accounts and measures, we're going to make history tonight as it looks like the early results are in."

A picture of Dungberry and Whiteman are now flashed up on the screen.

"None of our campaign experts thought that this day would come when the voting public would support not only a Libertarian for president, but a Native American for vice president.

"CNN projects that Dungberry has reached the super majority of delegates needed to win the presidency. Your new 45th President of the United States is John Dungberry!!" Blitzer announces.

"Our new Vice President is Barry Whiteman, a Native American from the great state of Washington."

Dungberry was at his campaign office when his cell phone was blowing up; friends, family and other colleagues were all calling to congratulate him.

"Oh my God!!" Dungberry said. He had to almost scream into his cell phone because of all the celebrations going on around him by his field workers.

He had one ear plugged so that he could hear the person on the other end. That person on the other end of the cell phone was Barack Obama, who called to congratulate him on running a positive election campaign and to wish him luck the next four years.

"Yes, Mr. President...oh...ok...yeah... I mean....yes, Barack, I look forward to meeting with you in the next few hours, sir! Thanks again for giving me a call and good luck on your next endeavors too!"

Dungberry hit the 'end' button on his iPhone 7 and placed it on the table in front of him. He raised his arms up in the 'victory position'.

"Woooooo hoooooo! Yeeeehaw!! We got it everyone!!!" Dungberry yelled out. The entire office went to a complete hush. There were several boxes of Kleenex that were being passed around as many people were crying with tears of joy.

Dungberry stood up on one of the desks to address his entire team.

"Please, please, no cell phone recordin's at this time. I want this moment to be just between you and me. Ya' know, 300 days ago, no one, I mean no one but you and I had any inclin' that we'd be in this position.

"No one gave us a snowball's chance in Texas that we'd be right here, right now, celebratin', cryin' tears of joy. In most people's eyes, it was a two-party race.

25

"Well, lookie what we've done ya'll….the Tortoise has won the race!!" The entire campaign office erupted with joy; more tears, more clapping, more hugging.

"You gave me blood!" *Someone in the audience yells 'Yeah!'*

"You gave me sweat!" *'Yeah!'*

"You would all take a bullet for me!" *'You got that right John!'*

"Well, dammit, we just won the White House! Now let's get to work!"

Again, the entire campaign office imploded and Dungberry hopped down off of the desk and began to give everyone around him hugs and high fives.

Chapter 3: Crying In Your Beer

The morning after the election, Donald Duckson woke up and put on his slippers. He still couldn't believe he didn't win the election. He didn't know if he was more upset or shocked that he lost or that neither him nor Republican Candidate Sherry Montgomery won the presidency.

He staggered into his restroom, closed the door and turned on the faucet. He splashed some water on his face and looked deep into his big blue eyes which had big black bags and circles around it.

There was a knock at the door.

"Sir? Sorry to bug you but you have a phone call," said his 'house assistant' Tomas (no 'h' in his name on purpose), an African American man in his 30's.

Donald turned off the water and wiped his face on a plush towel that was dangling from the wall. He opened the door and Tomas was standing there with a black handheld phone receiver.

"Thank you Tomas," Donald said and began to close the bathroom door.

"Oh sir, I just wanted to tell you," Tomas began to say and was interrupted by Donald.

"That's okay young man, I'm sure I'll figure out my next moves soon," Donald said nodding and closing the door slowly again.

Tomas impeded the door from closing by putting his hand out. "No, sir, I was going to say that I'll be moving out tomorrow."

"Tomorrow?" Donald asked.

"Yes sir, I will be getting my new keys to my condo in the morning. I have already begun to.."

"..tomorrow?" Donald interrupted him and repeated himself.

After a short pause Tomas said, "yes, sir,...tomorrow."

"You can't possibly get a condo this quickly? The election results were just last night!"

"I know Sir, I voted," Tomas said with a proud smile on his face.

"...well thank you for your vote and I'm sorry it didn't go..."

Tomas interrupted Donald: "Oh, sir, no, I didn't vote for you. I voted for John Dungberry."

"You did!" Donald said in an accusatory way.

"Yes sir, ...you see, he resonated with me and my entire family way more than you or Miss Sherry did sir."

Donald stood there with a stunned look on his face.

Tomas grabbed the door knob and began to slowly inch the door shut.

Back at Sherry's house, she was pouring her first cup of coffee for the day. The TV was already turned on. MSNBC was broadcasting a post-elections special where everything they said was 'Breaking News.'

She yawned and took a sip of her hot black coffee from her "lucky" mug, which was a white mug with the words 'LUCKY YOU' on the side of it. The 14 oz. mug was a gift from her sister Janet who at the time was referring to a lucky streak where she won over $20,000 during a weekend visit to Las Vegas before Sherry was in politics.

"We're still in shock over last night's US Presidential Election where Libertarian candidates John Dungberry and Barry Whiteman shook the world with a landslide victory over Sherry

Montgomery and Donald Duckson," said MSNBC News Anchor Alex Witt.

"That's right Alex, the world is still recovering from the news that our 45th President of the United States is from the Libertarian Party," said Chris Matthews, the second MSNBC News Anchor.

"Both Montgomery and Duckson teams have to be scratching their heads as to what went wrong with how they allowed the United States' first-ever non-Democratic or non-Republican party candidate to take the cake.

"Let's hope they are not crying in their beers this morning," Matthews said, shaking his head in disbelief.

Anger began to boil in Sherry's blood. She took the hot cup of coffee and slammed it to the ground next to her. The spilled coffee splattered all over her and she began to bounce up and down as if she was standing on hot rocks. She began to cry with pain from the hot coffee.

Her spouse came into the kitchen and attempted to console his grieving wife. As he approached her, he slipped on the hot coffee and the temperature from the coffee burned his back and the hand that he used to break the fall.

To the spoils are the victors and as the 45th President of the United States, John Dungberry woke up, he too was just like the other Presidential candidates, tired and exhausted. He was extremely happy, however, that he got the delegates he needed to secure the biggest win he'd ever get in his entire life.

As he awoke, his wife was sitting next to his bed as if she was watching him breathe in and out while sleeping.

Her presence startled him.

"What the hell you doin' Martha?" he said, sitting straight up.

"I'm just so proud of you my dear," she replied, clasping her hands and folding them into her lap.

She stood up and went over to the bed and began to climb on top of him. Her frail, 65-year-old white body covered in a pristine flowery dress began to drape the 67-year old President. She began to kiss him on his neck and tried to open the buttons on his pajama top.

He stopped her: "Honey, honey...now, I haven't even had my first cup 'a coffee!...What's gotten into you?"

She lay next to him and took a deep breath. "I've always wanted to make love to a President, ever since Lyndon B. Johnson was in office. That man had such a way about him!"

He slowly stood up from his lying down position and put on his robe. His wife, got up and straightened out her day dress, went to the mirror and fixed her hair. She walked up next to him and pinched his butt.

"Next time, Mr. President," she said winking at him and using her best Marilyn Monroe voice.

He tied his robe around his waist and slid his feet into his plush slippers. He went down stairs, hand-in-hand with his wife.

Light bulbs began popping around the dining room as reporters from all over the world were invited in to interview the President-elect during his first breakfast as President. The idea to have the press over during their "first breakfast" was Dungberry's idea. He felt that since they broke the mold of being the first Libertarians to win the White House, why not break the mold on other things?

He waved his hand at the photographers as he and the First Lady crept down their long stair case. As he was negotiating the stairs and waving at his invited paparazzi, he somehow missed the last step and both he and his wife went tumbling down onto the wooden floor.

The two Secret Servicemen who were standing at the bottom of the stairs tried to catch the two but instead, they ended up colliding with the two of them causing a four-person pileup.

Flash bulbs went off as the photographers were having a field day with what just happened. CNN was broadcasting live:

"Oh my God, the President just fell!" Wolfe Blitzer exclaimed as he was broadcasting the events inside their home live on-the-air.

"Are they okay?" Blitzer said looking off-camera and listening to his producer who was speaking to him through his ear-piece.

"Okay, it looks as though the two of them are okay," Blitzer said and took a deep breath.

A minute later, Dungberry made his way over to the long dining table where a series of hot plates were waiting for him and his wife. He sat down and the paparazzi enclosed the space around the table.

"Now, I want to apologize for that little fall over there by the stairs," Dungberry said as he grabbed his wife's hand. "I guess you can say we FALL in love with each other every morning."

The reporters were all nodding their heads and smiling all cheesy at what Dungberry just said.

"Her love and support for me continues to FLOOR me....

"I guess you can say that was my FIRST TRIP as President...

"Guess I better learn to ROLL with the punches?"

With each statement Dungberry said, the reporters all laughed along with him; some laughs were true and most were fake.

Meanwhile, that night Donald Duckson was finishing up having dinner with his wife and kids. His phone chirped and there was a new text message:

"Still reeling from yesterday's defeat?"

'Who and the hell would write that?' Donald thought to himself.

He noticed the phone number was a DC area code and wrote back:

Who is this?

A text message came back:

Your DPIC..

He wrote back:

Huh?

A new text came in:

Your defeated partner in crime.

Automatically he knew it was Sherry.

A new text came in to Donald's phone:

Heading to 'The Spot'.

The Spot was the bar that all of the elected officials hung out in downtown Washington DC, but it wasn't the premiere place that she was heading to. Instead, the people that were with the new President would occupy a bar called "The Brass Ring," a club/bar, that you had to be a member of.

Now Sherry and Donald were both members of the The Brass Ring, but tonight, Sherry wanted to go to a place where she would not be spotted by Dungberry's entourage of supporters.

She had something up her sleeve and she wanted to talk to Donald one-on-one.

Donald entered "The Spot" and saw Sherry sitting by herself at the bar. She was holding her cell phone in her right hand and punching in letters and numbers with her right thumb. She had an 18 oz. cold beer in front of her.

"No crying in our beers?" Donald said standing directly behind her.

She twisted around her skinny, frail body and gave him a big hug.

"Nice campaign sir," she said looking up from her hugging position.

"You too young lady," he said looking down.

If you didn't know the two people, you'd think they were a couple. That was always the way they were towards each other in private, which to onlookers, made the fact that they were literally at each other's throats just a month ago so puzzling.

Donald sat down next to Sherry and ordered up his usual 25-year Glenn Livet scotch, in a glass cup with two pieces of ice. Of course there were more expensive scotch selections available but he was an old-fashion guy.

Mess with the way he conducts business, that's okay, but don't mess with his scotch or 'old reliable' as he called it.

After all of the niceties were given to each other, a stern look came onto Sherry's face. "We lost! Let's just start by saying that!"

"Looks like you may have started an hour or so, how many have you had?" Donald asked referring to the number of drinks she consumed so far.

"You're not my father, so just listen up," she said.

He looked down at his icy glass of buttery smooth goodness and let her talk.

"We need to pull up our big girl panties and figure out our next move," she said

"Next move? What next move? I was planning on taking the wife and heading to the Bahamas for a sweet little trip down there for the next oh, say, ...4 years or so."

She looked very puzzled. "Huh?"

"Sure, I'm not going to stay here and be a member of society when we have a hick from Ohio and 'Skin from...God, where is he from again?" Donald asked as he took a swig from his glass.

"Tula...Tulip...No...Tula..." Sherry tried to mutter out the word Tu-lay-lip (Tulalip).

"Well, wherever in God's creation he's from, I'm not going to be apart of it!" he said and swallowed the rest of his 3 oz. cup of scotch. He began to use his teeth to crunch on the ice.

"We need to band together and become a super team in 2020!" she exclaimed.

"What?" Donald asked.

"Sure, why not? Sherry rhetorically replied.

"They shocked the world with the first Libertarian and first Injun to occupy the White House, why couldn't we be the first 'cross-the-aisle' candidates to win the Presidency?" she asked.

"That's just ludicrous," Donald said.

"So you're not in?" Sherry asked.

"I didn't say that," Donald said looking up at the bar tender and gestured over to her that he needed another drink.

The bartender came over and poured him another gratuitous glass of scotch and his signature two pieces of ice. As the two pieces of ice were being dropped into his cup, she said:

"You see, two is better than one!" She stood up, staggered in place and kissed the older man on his unshaven cheek.

She slowly stood up and staggered out of the bar as he watched her negotiate gravity.

"Better call her an Uber?" the bartender suggested to Donald.

He stood up and ran out of the bar to ensure she didn't drive home in her condition.

CHAPTER 4: GETTING ALL CHOKED UP

A week later, Dungberry invited several key people to the White House for a party to thank them for their support. As each guest walked into the White House, they were met by a person behind a table to check them in.

A large van pulled into the driveway leading up to the White House. Out came 9 Native Americans, Tulalip tribal members, each in their traditional Coast Salish regalia. The van was supposed to be white, but through time it had worn out and some of the paint was chipped and parts of the paint were rusted out.

The van was meant for only 7 people so for the past 4 days as it traveled from Tulalip, WA to Washington, DC., they would have to stop; not only for a potty break but for a 'stretch break.'

The nine people were Vice President Barry Whiteman's closest relatives as he was allowed 9 total tickets to Dungberry's 200. A valet host came running down the driveway and seeing him run towards them, Uncle Jack, Barry's eldest living relative, took out his cane and started to wave it around him to ward off the oncoming young man who was just there to park the van.

"You get the hell away from us...you! you..!...We're here to see my nephew!!" Uncle Jack yelled out into the dusk-dusted night. The young Italian valet host stopped dead in his tracks and put out his hands in peace.

"Uncle,..Uncle, it's okay...he's here to help us," Deb, Barry's first-cousin said. Uncle Jack put away his cane and waved his hand at the young man as if to say 'oh, to hell with you.'

Uncle Jack, Deb, Barry's other first-cousins Charlie, Liz, Tammy, Gary, and his auntie Georgianna and auntie-mom Zeta started making their way up the driveway towards the White House. As they entered, a 6'3" African-American woman in a dress suit welcomed them in.

"My name is Louise, may I see your ID?" she asked them.

"What did she say?!" Auntie Georgianna said, loud enough to get the attention of others who were checking in as well.

"She is asking for our IDs, Auntie,.." said Gary.

"WHAT FOR?!" yelled Georgianna again, interrupting her grand - nephew.

"'Cause, that's the rules." Gary said smiling now as he was digging into his pants pockets to find his wallet.

"Rules! Don't they know who we're with?" Georgianna asked.

Deb came over and patted her grand auntie on the back: "Yes, Auntie, they know. Now let's just get our IDs out okay?"

Deb opened up her Aunties' purses and got their IDs and grabbed her first-cousins' IDs and stacked them together and handed it to the host.

A puzzled look came across Louise's face. "Uh, do you happen to have any other IDs? I don't recognize these ones," she said.

Deb's smiling face went from happy to angry. "Are you trying to embarrass us?" Deb pointed down at the IDs..."those IDs are more acceptable than the shitty Washington State IDs that you're probably wanting to see. We have a Government-to-Government relationship with the United States that YOU MUST HONOR!...

Gary seeing his cousin begin to fling her long black hair at the White House team member, intervened and pulled her away from the African American woman.

"Stand over there cuz, or else we may be spending our time in jail," he said grimacing. He dusted off his hands and straightened out his bolo tie. "Now, there must be something we can do to straighten this whooole thing out."

"Yes, we need to see different IDs, please," Louise said with a deep breath. "State-issued IDs and passports would work just fine. It said so on your invitations, right?"

"Invitations? Uh, no we didn't get an invitation in the mail or email," Gary said.

"Inv-it-ations? We don't use no stupid invit-a-shuns!!" Liz intervened. Liz and Charlie both were the family 'social-ites'. Don't call them the family drunks, or else risk losing your life by their hands. No, they are the *social-ites* who spend their days and nights enjoying their 21st Amendment right to drink.

Barry specifically asked Deb and Gary to watch his first-cousins to keep them from drinking as they got to the White House, and in fact, that was the deal he made with them two in order for them to be able to attend the gala.

"Then how did you know about this event ma'am?" Louise asked Liz.

"Uh, we actually *talk* to our brother, that's how!" Liz said as she started to take her high heels off.

Gary came over to his cousin Liz: "Come on now, cuzzie, you're only making it more difficult. Let's just get our cousin Barry and have him settle this. Louise, will you do us a solid and ask our cousin Barry to come out and help settle this with you?"

"Oh, the Vice President is your cousin?" Louise asked.

"Now you're all nice to us?!" Liz rhetorically asked rolling her eyes.

"Let me get someone on the phone, I'll be right back," Louise said as she turned around and walked into a group of White House team members, including security and Secret Service.

"You better watch your back!" Liz yelled at Louise whose back was now turned to them.

"Alright, alright..now, let's all just settle the fuck down! We are here for cousin Barry and we don't want to mess this up for him alright?" Gary asked.

All eight of them were silent and nodded their heads.

Louise came back and had her hands in a clasped position. "I am very, very, very sorry everyone for the mix up. We are more than happy to welcome you to the White House as a guest of the Vice President."

She sidestepped out of the way and ushered them through security and into the main lobby of the White House.

All nine of them were in awe of the sheer size and vastness of the entire space.

"They got a can around here?" Auntie Georgianna said in her normal voice, which was a few decibel levels louder than everyone else's.

Louise came over to them from her normal 'greeting' position near the front entrance and guided Auntie Georgianna to the nearest restroom. As the eight of them were waiting for her to come back to them so that they could continue the journey towards the East Room, where past Presidents hosted most of the events and entertainment over the hundred years that it was there.

Auntie Georgianna opened the restroom door and locked it behind her. She lifted up her long dress, pulled her bloomers down and sat on the toilet and took a deep breath. As she exhaled a large quantity of feces came out. She began to sing a traditional song: 'hey ya,...ye' hey, ya'...more feces came out.

Louise knocked on the door. "Are you okay in there?" Another attendant came over to Louise. "It sounds like she is crying in there....Hello?? Are you okay?" Louise was now concerned.

More traditional singing continues....

Almost 10 minutes later, Auntie Georgianna came out of the restroom. She had some toilet paper stuck to the back of her leg, which also had some fecal matter on it.

Seeing the toilet paper, Louise ran up to Georgianna. "Uh, ma' am...you've got...you've got.."

"WHAT??! NOW WHAT??!" Georgianna, walking towards her family like a locomotive stopped and exclaimed.

Not trying to cause more of a scene, Louise decided just to pluck the toilet paper off of her leg and be done with it. As she pulled it off and began to crinkle it up to throw it into the waste basket, she felt something wet and creamy. Right away, she knew it wasn't a good thing; disposed of it and hustled into the restroom to wash up.

Inside the restroom, the toilet looked like Hurricane Sandy paid it a visit. There was toilet paper everywhere, the water from the bottom of the toilet had come up and poured onto the floor. After washing up, she radio'd housekeeping to come and clean up the mess.

Now that all nine of them were back together again, they continued their long trek to the East Room. Since they had the two elders with them, they all had to stop and wait every 10 steps to give them time to catch their breath.

"Why and the hell can't they give me a piggy back or something?" Uncle Jack asked.

"We're almost there Uncle," Gary said. "You're doing real good Unc!"

"Oh fuck you and your little young legs. What I wouldn't give right now to have those scrawny, women-like legs to be able to walk around in," Uncle Jack replied.

Gary just smiled and looked around while he waited for the elders to start moving again.

Finally, they arrived to the East Room where another host was there to greet them. The host asked them for their names and proceeded to walk them to their table which was up in the front near the large stage that was placed there and had a podium on it.

The nine of them sat down and each were greeted with their own server. The server came over and introduced themselves to each of the nine people.

"Wow, this is cool," Liz said. "We got our own server? Ooohhh.. mine is a hottie!"

Her server came back and asked her if she wanted a glass of Chardonnay.

"Oh, hell yeah,....keep pouring,...keep pouring...good!" Liz instructed.

They each were given hot wash cloths to wipe on their foreheads and hands. Uncle Jack used his inside his shirt so that it would help relieve some arthritis he had on his shoulder.

A little over 20 minutes later, Barry finally arrived. He entered the East Room and made a b-line to his guests' table. He got to the table and bent down to give his elders a hug a first. His Uncle Jack hugged him and his Auntie Georgianna kissed him on his cheek; Auntie Zeta who was the quiet one of Georgianna's sisters hugged him too.

"I'm so very proud of you, son," Auntie Z said and Barry returned her comment with a smile back to her.

His first cousins all stood up and one by one they hugged their cousin.

A server of his own came over and pulled out a chair for the Vice President. He sat down and looked around.

"Well, how was the trip out here from good ol' WA State?" Barry asked.

"Good...good..I mean it took us a lot longer to get out here but we made it, that's all that counts," Gary said.

"If you hadn't used your God-damn flip phone to get us here, we might've got here a lot sooner!" Liz said.

Barry whispered into Gary's ear: "Are they (short pause) okay?"

"Oh, Liz and Charlie? Oh yeah, they're doing just fine," Gary assured him.

"No, I mean, are they intoxicated?" Barry asked.

Gary looked over at Liz and her and Charlie were sitting next to each other. Charlie was talking to Liz and by the looks of it *their* party was getting better and better with each passing minute and each glass of wine they consumed.

"Nah, cuz, they're okay." Gary said again.

Barry nodded his head and pushed his chair into the table a little bit closer.

A voice came over the public address speakers inside the East Room.

"I'd like to welcome you all here to the Shock of the Century Victory Party,..." said the public address announcer.

"Is that... Is that...is that Justin Bieber?" Liz asked. She took another big gulp of her wine.

Barry nodded his head.

"Now, you're all probably wondering what the hell is Justin Bieber doing here in the White House and moreover, why is he emceeing this event?" Bieber said. He was wearing a white tuxedo with a black and white polka dot bow tie and no sleeves on his tuxedo jacket or undershirts, exposing his very tanned, very athletic arms.

"I LOVE YOU BEEBZ!!" Liz stood up and yelled.

"I love you too momma," Bieber immediately replied back. Liz sat back down and took another big gulp of her white wine.

"I'm here tonight to celebrate the win of the century. Raise your hands right now if you truly, truly believed that a President from Ohio or better yet, a Vice President running-mate from a reservation would win this or any Presidential election in our lifetime!!" Bieber said smiling from ear-to-ear.

A few hands were raised, none from Barry 's table.

"C'mon guys, you could at least raise your hands!!" Barry said.

Only Gary and Deb's hands raised from their table and Barry just shook his head in disgust.

"Let's be honest, I don't think we'll ever see this again....EVER! So let's party like fuckin' rock stars tonight and celebrate the fact that we have two of the best men, two natural born leaders, two men who will lead this country like it's never been lead before!"

The entire room now filled with over 1,000 people all stood up and applauded. Again, only Deb, Gary and Barry stood up from their table.

"Now, I'd like to introduce you to the man of the hour. He really needs no introduction, let's give a round of applause to your 45th President, Mr. John Dungberry!!"

Dungberry stood up from his table, which was one table up towards the stage than Barry 's table. He pushed in his chair and ran up the small staircase leading up to the stage. He shook Bieber's hand and gave him a large bear hug, exposing Bieber's muscles.

He stepped up to the podium and began talking on the microphone:

"Yee haw! What an introduction huh? How about a round of applause for Justin 'Freakin' Bieber!" John exclaimed.

"The Bieb's is right. Who'da thunk it that two men from the great Libertarian party would win the Presidential election! Let's not dwell on the fact that this was one of the lowest voter turnouts in the history of our elections. Let's not dwell on the fact that most people didn't trust the Democratic or Republican candidates or their rhetoric. Instead, let's focus on the fact that the US voters spoke and they spoke LOUD and FRICKIN' clear! They wanted change and a change is what we bring!!" Dungberry said with a loud appreciative response from the audience.

"Before we go any further, I need to bring up to the stage, a person that I call a dear friend. Someone that I believed in so long ago and someone who I know if I was ever in a pinch, I could call in a jiffy!" Dungberry said leaning on the podium with both arms.

Barry slid himself away from his table and stood up, buttoned up his jacket and was preparing to go up on stage.

"That person is my wife, YOUR first lady and the only lady in my life, FIRST LADY Martha Dungberry!!"

44

Barry sat back down in his chair in embarrassment.

After she got up to say her small speech, the President finished his speech and did not make mention of his running mate, Barry.

"What the hell is going on cuzzie, how come he didn't introduce you?" Deb asked. "Are they ever going to introduce you or are you just their token Indian? Hell, I'll go up there right now and introduce you my damn self!" Deb started to take her heels and her earrings off.

"No! No! Deb, just sit right there, it will be okay," Barry said. Trying to get their attention to something else Barry said "Anyone wish for a dinner roll?"

The First Lady spoke and the entire time, Barry's cousins were all getting restless wondering when their cousin was going to be able to go up on stage to say a few words.

After dinner was over, Barry excused himself to go use the restroom. He walked by the President's table and he could tell that Dungberry and his entourage were heavily intoxicated already.

Barry waved at the President and the President flashed his smile at him, showing his purple teeth from the red wine that he had been drinking since before dinner came out.

"Man, that food was deee-licous!!" Uncle Jack said. "Time to pray to the Gods!"

Praying to the Gods in most cultures meant going to Mass or holding hands while they said Grace or even kneeling on the ground and communicating with their Creator. Uncle Jack's and Auntie Georgianna's version of this was very, let's just say 'different'.

Uncle Jack pulled out his man-purse that he had strapped to his right shoulder and opened it up. He pulled out a small pipe, unrolled the sack that contained a gram of marijuana and pushed it into the pipe.

"C'mon brother, light that mother fucker up!" Auntie Georgianna exclaimed.

"Hold your damn horses little sissy...I'll get this goin' in no time!" Uncle Jack replied.

He took the pipe and a cigar lighter and lit the pipe up, engulfing the pipe with a very large flame that enveloped the head of the pipe. The once dark green weed was now becoming orange and black. A large white puff of smoke exited Uncle Jack's mouth up into the air.

Dungberry, sitting at his table, was just taking a large bite of his thick juicy London broil steak when he smelled something different. He turned around and saw Uncle Jack light the pipe and was shocked.

With a mouthful of London broil, he tried to get his wife's attention. He was pointing at Barry's table but his wife was listening to a story by Jaida Pinkett Smith, whom she had grown close to during the campaign and who was sitting next to her.

The steak that was in the President's mouth was about to go into his belly and he would expose his running mate's family as drug addicts thus kicking his Vice President out of the White House when a piece of steak got stuck in his windpipe.

He began choking and thumping his chest, trying to dislodge it from his body. His face began to turn red and water came out of his eyes. He had enough of a reach to hit his wife on her shoulders trying to get her attention.

She waved his initial thumping on her shoulder away as if to say 'quit being rude.' Finally, after 30 seconds, she turned around and saw that her husband was turning blue.

"OH MY GOD!!" she yelled at the top of her lungs. "Medics!! Medics!!"

Secret Servicemen came out of nowhere and began to do the Heimlich maneuver on him.

"C'mon you son of a bitch, breathe!!" said a secret serviceman.

Seeing all of the people over at the President's table, Barry ran from the entrance of the East Room towards the President.

"Oh my God, please help him!" Barry looked up and asked his Creator for help.

The secret servicemen took turns trying to revive the President.

"Oh, what the hell is goin' on over there, why can't a Native smoke in peace?" Uncle Jack asked, taking another puff of weed.

Barry went back to his table and politely but sternly asked his elders to put their "peace pipe" away. They concurred with his request and put the pipe into Auntie Georgianna's purse.

After 10 minutes of CPR and the Heimlich Maneuver, the 45th President of the United States was pronounced dead.

Barry sat down at his table and couldn't believe what just happened. Just as the announcement was made and all kinds of sadness spread across the East Room, about 20 secret servicemen swarmed Barry 's table and surrounded him.

"We need you to come with us right now!" said Tommy, the lead secret serviceman.

"Oh God, they're gonna arrest us Gee-Gee (Uncle's nickname for Auntie Georgianna) for smokin' the lettuce!" Uncle Jack yelled out.

Barry was lifted out of there by the secret service using a fireman's carry, he asked: "Where are we going?"

"You'll see!" Tommy said as they quickly escorted Barry out of the ballroom.

"Well that's a fine how do you do!" Charlie said, now very intoxicated. "Now what are we supposed to do?" He grabbed the bottle of wine that was on the table and took a big swig from it.

CHAPTER 5: FAKE IT TIL YOU MAKE IT

The Secret Service rushed Barry through the underground tunnels and into the basement of the White House called the Underground Command Center. This was White House emergency protocols, none of which Barry ever was briefed on.

A judge, a transcriber, a priest, the Secretary of Defense Ashton Granger and Department of Defense General were already down there awaiting Barry's arrival and the secret service.

"Alright Mr. Vice President, everything's in place," Granger said.

"In place for what?" Barry asked.

"This is no time for jokes Mr. Vice President," Granger said.

"No wait a damn minute!! What is going on??!!" Barry asked.

"Mr. Vice President, John was pronounced dead and you are now being positioned as our new President of the United States," explained Granger.

Barry dropped to his knees in disbelief. "You have to be shitting me!"

"Nope,..now get up and let's get this moving." Granger said helping Barry up from his squatted position on the floor.

Granger motioned to the judge who was standing against a wall of television monitors which showed every angle of the White House's interior and exterior boundaries.

"Okay, now please repeat after me," Judge Knowles said. "Raise your right hand and .."

"Raise your right hand..." Barry started to echo the judge.

"Um, no, Mr. Vice President..." the judge said.

"Um, no, Mr. Vice President...." Barry said.

Granger stepped in between them and whispered into Barry's ear: "Raise your right hand and when he starts the oath, that is when you repeat after him, okay?"

Barry gave him a very Presidential head nod, as if to say 'Got it!'

"Okay, let's try this again," the judge said taking a deep breath. "I Do Solemnly swear that I will faithfully execute..."

"I do solemnly? ....solemn-leeeee...swear..." Barry paused as he couldn't remember the next word that the judge said.

"that I will faithfully execute..." the judge repeated.

"that I will....I will...I will," Barry began to stammer.

"Faithfully?" the judge said.

"Faithfully?" Barry asked in a question.

Granger stepped in once again and whispered into Barry's ear. "It's not a question, it's a statement."

Barry once again gave him a confident head nod.

He looked over at Granger who was back standing in his original spot: "Faithfully!.."

Granger gave him a stern head nod as if to say: Hell Yeah!"

The judge continued: "execute the Office of the President of the United States."

"execute the Office of the President of the United States," Barry said as he started to do a little dance to gain rhythm.

"and will to the best of my ability"...the judge said.

"and WILL to the BEEEEST of my ABILITY..." said Barry, now spinning in a circle as if he was Michael Jackson "preserve," the judge said now resorting to one word sentences, just to get through this more easier.

"PRESERVE!!!"

"protect"

"PROTECT!!!"

"and defend"

"AND DEEEEEFENNNND!"

"the Constitution of the United States!"

"the Constitution of the United States!...Yeeehaw!!"

Barry and the rest of the people in the Underground Command Center all took a collective sigh of relief. They didn't get a real chance to grieve the untimely death of the former leader of the free world.

Barry had a feeling that from here on out, he was going to have to fake it until he made it. I mean, who else would bet that within a week of taking the Presidential Oath, that he would become the next President of the free world?

Just as emotion was about to set in with all of them, Ursula Tally, US Press Secretary came into the room.

"Okay it's all set up," Tally said.

"What's all set up?" Barry asked.

"The press conference, there are over 300 journalists all waiting with recorders in hand to hear what you have to say," she explained.

"300?....Reporters?..." a white sheet covered Barry 's dark complexion. He sat down to catch his breath.

"You got this, Mr. President," Tally said.

"Hey, you're the first one to call me that," Barry said.

Tally stood up straight.."Hey, that's cool, I was the first one to call him President...anyway, we need to get out there so, I've developed some talking points for you to say, okay?"

She handed him a three-ring binder that had two sheets of paper in it. The font on each line was very big, 24-point font, which made it easier for the 53-year-old to read.

He went through each bullet point and as he read each one he nodded his head in approval. He got to the fourth bullet point and raised his hand.

"Uh, sir, you don't have to raise your hand, you can just talk," Granger said.

A slightly embarrassed Barry said: "Oh, well, here it says that John had a heart attack, not that he had choked to death?"

"We can't have history say that the strongest, most powerful person in the world died from choking on a London broil!!" Granger said.

"But that's exactly what happened!" Barry said.

Barry stood up and began to address the small group that was in the Command Center. "We have the..no wait, we owe it, to the people of this great Nation to tell the truth! Even when that truth hurts us, we need to say it and I know that our beloved John would've wanted it that way," Barry said.

There was a complete silence in the room.

"Okay, Mr. President, I will change that in the teleprompter," Tally said.

"And no more teleprompters..we're going to do this the Native way, without bullet points, without teleprompters, we're going to talk *TO* our people, and not *down* to them. I've read the bullet points and I have these words plugged into my head and my heart and I will now go out and address them to the world."

Barry threw the three-ring binder down on an empty table and exited the Command Center. The rest of the people in the room stood there looking at each other.

Barry came back into the room: "Now, how and the hell do I get out of here?!!"

Inside the White House Briefing Room, just as Tally said, there were over 300 people in there anxiously waiting what news that needed to be said. Someone in the dinner gala just a few minutes before Barry got into the briefing room leaked a tweet: *"The President is Dead".*

Just as he entered the room, flash bulbs went off and a huge clamor of words started to barrage the 46th President. Barry stepped up to the podium and right away, he was shocked at how many people were in the room. He saw all of the big cameras, the TV cameras; a drone had fallen from the ceiling and was now eye level with the President. Fear had built up inside him and he had no words.

"Um...um...um..." the President said.

Tally, noticing that he had got star struck, gently handed him his three-ring binder.

The President acknowledged her and she politely gave him a big smile. He opened the three-ring binder and put his glasses on.

He looked down and placed his right index finger on the first bullet. Line-by-line, he went through the briefing that Tally had prepared. When it got time to say the fourth bullet, he went as scripted and did not tell the American public the actual truth.

Even though he didn't like the late-President, he had respect for his position. At 'the moment of truth,' he decided that he would tell a little white lie to protect the Oval Office, the integrity of the system and save that story for another day.

As he finished the briefing, he decided to let Tally take on the extra questions that the media had for him. With a saddened look on his face, he made a b-line directly to the exit, stage left.

The President got back into the Oval Office and his Executive Assistant Dena Montana followed him into the space.

"Please find my family and get them up here as soon as possible?" the President directed.

"Yes, sir I will find them right away sir," she said. "And sir, I want to congratulate you and tell you that I am here for you in our country's time of need."

"Thanks Dena, I sincerely appreciate you." he said.

She exited the room and the phone rang. He went over to the desk and he was looking for the phone. The phone rang again and again, some four or five times when Dena came rushing in.

"Sir, I didn't show you how to use the phone, I'm sorry. Our phone in this room is not like the traditional phone we grew up with. Instead, it's a video phone and here is the remote," she handed him the remote and pushed the 'Accept' button that was on it.

The next morning, Barry woke up on the second floor of the White House in his bedroom. It was 8:30 AM on a Monday morning and he did his usual routine.

His bedroom was the size of his entire Washington D.C. apartment and bigger than 90% of the homes back on the Tulalip reservation. He stood up from his bed and opened up the curtains to his room.

Outside, in the Fall-weather, looking down on the backyard grounds, there were gardeners raking leaves and in the distance he could see a crew of men lifting one of the statues so that the other ones could pressure wash underneath it.

He opened the door to his room and entered a commons area where there is a sofa, bookshelves filled with books, lamps, and a small table.

He opened up one of the doors that lead out to the backyard and stepped out onto the deck that overlooked the entire area.

He yawned and did a huge cat stretch. As he finished yawning and stretching, he looked down and a group of housekeepers were outside shaking some small area carpets out, dusting them. One of them stopped and nudged the other ones and pointed up at Barry.

Barry, not trying to be rude began to wave at them and the other housekeepers started to laugh, a few of them covering their smiles.

He wondered why they were laughing and when he looked down to the left, he saw the gardeners all stop raking away at the leaves that was down below him.

It wasn't until a small breeze blew through the courtyard that he felt very 'open'; *he wasn't wearing any clo*thes. His dark skin turned a 'beet' red and covered his shriveled genitals and he slowly crept backwards into the commons area.

As he entered in, a few of Barry's family members walked in on him and his bare naked body. Barry began to run back into his room and slammed the door behind him.

"Boy, it wasn't like I didn't see that white butt all your baby years!" Auntie Georgianna yelled out. Georgianna, Jack and Deb all sat on the nice sofas that was in the common area.

A few minutes later, with a robe on, Barry came out. "Hey guys, ...sorry about that."

"That's okay cuz, I guess you're not used to living in such a public place?" Deb asked him. Barry nodded.

"Well, this whole thing is just a whirlwind of a time isn't it, Neph?" Uncle Jack asked.

"Yeah, I'm not too sure what to do next..."Barry said.

"Not sure?! Boy, what the hell is wrong with you. You come from a legacy of leaders and it's about time this country is led by an Indian!" Auntie Georgianna reminded him. "You go in there and put some presidential clothes on and go get to work!"

Barry started to feel better about being the President of the United States. Auntie Georgianna's words were becoming more and more inspirational; a sort of 'kick-you-in-your-pants or light your ass on fire' type of talk.

He stood up.

"That's right, cuz, you are a leader, a born leader, one that we all look up to. You helped take our tribe from nothing to well...a little more than nothing, you became a great leader for the State of Washington, now let's go show them white people a thing or two about how we do it in Indian Country!" Deb said.

Barry raised his hands as if he just hit all 10 bowling pins for a strike. "Now Go!" Deb said and pointed back into his room.

Barry jumped up and down and started to go towards his room when his right toe stubbed the table and he went tumbling down to the ground, exposing his white butt again.

He hopped up and gave the thumbs up that he was okay and he went backwards into his room and gave a wave to his family as he closed the door.

He put on a nice suit and bolo tie, brushed his long black hair free of any knots and headed downstairs towards the Oval Office.

As he entered the hallway leading up to the Oval Office, he was hit with over 30 people all waiting for him to answer questions they have, give direction or just simple updates that they normally give the Commander in Chief.

"Whoa, who the hell are all these people?" Barry asked Executive Assistant Dena.

"These, Mr. President, are the people who were here since 6 AM to see you," Dena said, looking up, over her reading glasses up at Barry.

"6AM? Who does business that damn early?" Barry asked.

The noise from the shouting got a bit deafening, so Barry turned around to quiet them all down.

"Everyone! Everyone!" Barry exclaimed just above the noise. "I am extremely sorry for my tardiness; I promise that will change going forward. Now, Miss Dena, who was here first?"

"David Youngster from the International Affairs division was here first," Dena replied.

"Okay, Mr. David, come on in and let's get started," Barry said, pointing in front of him towards the Oval Office. "And Dena, thank you for setting me straight."

Barry was able to listen to all 30 people who were waiting for him and by now it was almost 3 PM. He hadn't had any breakfast or lunch and was starting to get 'hangry'.

He pushed the intercom button on the phone and asked Dena to arrange lunch for him in 30 minutes out on the patio of the Oval Office.

"What would you like to eat Mr. President?" Dena asked.

"Do we have anyone that can cook up a nice ghoulash?" Barry asked.

"Uh, ghoul-ash? What is that Mr. President?" Dena was puzzled.

"Okay, never mind that. How about an Indian Taco?" Barry's mouth started to water.

"I'm 0-for-2, Mr. President, I've never heard of that either." Dena confessed.

"Oh alright!! Fine!! Nevermind, just have someone whip me up a burger! Can you handle that??!!" Barry was now very 'hangry'.

"You got it Mr. President." Dena said.

"Are you ready for your next appointment sir?"

"Yes...(a short pause) and Dena?" Barry hesitated.

"Yes sir?" Dena replied.

"Sorry about shouting at you, I know you don't know how I operate yet and I am still figuring this whole thing out. Anyway, sorry." Barry apologized.

"No problem sir, I'm here for you when you need me." Dena said.

Barry's next appointment came into his office and they began to talk.

About 45-minutes later, a famished Barry went out to the patio and waiting there on a small oval table with a nice white table cloth was a plate with a hot cover on it, a yellow rose, folding napkin and silverware.

He sat down and had to figure out which fork to use. After navigating his way through the silverware he noticed a small envelope that was a bit camouflaged into the white table cloth.

It was a note from the Libertarian National Committee Chairperson, Natalie Heyland:

"Mr. President, welcome to your first day on the job. Let's get together soon to discuss some candidates to be your Vice President."

He opened up the hot cover and exposed the beautifully done cheeseburger and fries, cooked similarly to what you would find at an In-and-Out Burger restaurant.

Barry took the time to pray over his meal, thanking the Creator for the blessings he had and to bless the cooks of his meal.

About an hour after he ate the final bite of his hamburger and fries, his cell phone alerted him to his next meeting. He had his briefing with National Security Advisor Damon Rasmussen and his full team of assistants.

He stood up, went back into the Oval Office, grabbed his suit jacket and put it on. He grabbed his notepad and exited the Oval Office.

As he entered the War Room, everyone in the room stood up and gave him a warm welcome through clapping.

"Alright, alright..now, that's okay you guys, you don't need to clap for me," Barry said smiling from ear-to-ear. Quieting them down, he took his seat and everyone else also took theirs.

"Okay, let's get to work," Barry said. "Mr. Rasmussen, please give us today's security briefing?"

Damon Rasmussen, an Irishman from Boston, Massachusetts was a former lawyer and counsel to many big corporate entities around the world.

He decided to leave his law office about 5 years ago and was recruited by Dungberry just a week ago to take on the duties of National Security Advisor based on his track record of great relationships around the world and his law background.

"Thank you Mr. President," Rasmussen said, standing up and addressing the people in the rectangular shaped room. There were TV monitors and digital boards up all over the room, as well as a digi-writer monitor at the head of the table, which allowed anyone to use a pen to write over the contents on the screen.

Rasmussen, a short 5' 6" man with red hair and red mustache had on a grey suit and red tie. His blue eyes peered out of his gold and shiny rimmed glasses. He used a PowerPoint clicker to supplement his verbal update.

"It's been just a short week since I took this position that God rest his soul, Mr. Dungberry invited me to take. It's been an honor and a privilege to learn the information that I'm about to share with you today," Rasmussen said.

"As you can see on the screen, our first major threat is several terrorist threats that our intel is telling us that may be imminent.

"They are using all kinds of weapons that our Secretary of Defense is monitoring daily.

"Our second threat is, quite frankly, Mother Earth."

"Mother Earth?" Barry asked.

"Yes sir. The NOAA folks are heavily engaged in monitoring Hurricane Daniel, just off the coast of Texas where they have endured quite a bit of rain and floods already.

"Finally, our last major threat to security is in Columbia. As most of us know in this room, the Columbians are the ones who currently produce the world's largest poppy seeds, which in return make 90% of the world's heroin.

"Addiction to heroin is on the rise in the United States---major rise than it has ever been, Mr. President, that is why I have it as one of our top three security issues we must address soon."

Barry sat and listened to the rest of Rasmussen's presentation and asked a few questions here and there to get better clarified on what he was presenting.

The three-hour meeting lasted until about 9 PM, when Barry decided enough was enough. He retreated back up to his room and easily fell asleep.

The next morning, he woke up around 4 AM and decided that he needed to start his day way earlier than what he was normally doing prior to becoming the President.

Breakfast was ready for him at 6 AM and he enjoyed freshly cooked eggs and bacon, toast and coffee. He read several newspapers from the Washington DC area and took some time to pray.

At 7:30 AM, he got his calendar briefing from Dena and one-by-one, he sat and listened to the 30 or so people who needed to see him, some people from yesterday and some that were newly acquainted with the President.

It wasn't until his 10 AM meeting that it dawned on him that he hadn't seen his family since yesterday morning.

"Dena, where the heck are my family members? Crap!" Barry exclaimed over the intercom.

"They have been on a tour of the greater DC area," she said.

"Who arranged that?" Barry asked.

"I did sir," she replied.

"Wow, you're good!" he said.

"I know I am, sir," a confident Dena said in reply.

"Okay, please arrange dinner for us out near my bedroom please?" Barry asked.

"Anything in particular you want served sir?" she asked.

"Um..hmm...how about some fresh salmon, potatoes, green salad and some frybread?" he asked.

"Sounds good," Dena said.

"You know what frybread is Miss Dena?" Barry asked.

"Yes sir, I've been Google-ing all kinds of Native American foods since you stumped me yesterday," she said.

"Yup, you're good Miss Dena, you're damn good!" he complimented her.

Later that night, Barry entered the commons area near his bedroom where he asked Dena to set up the dinner for him and his family.

Liz stood up, jokingly and said "All rise, the honorable Barry Whiteman, President of the United States!"

"Sit your flat ass down," Uncle Jack instructed.

The smile from Liz's face went from big to now a scowl directed at her uncle.

"He's right, Liz, you all don't need to stand up, let's eat?" Barry asked.

"Sorry I'm late, had a meeting that ran later than I expected," Barry said.

"It's about time you showed up, just smelling all this good food made me want to just jump right in," said Barry's Auntie Zeta.

"You all could've eaten if you wanted to?" Barry said.

"How was your day cuzzie?" Tammy asked.

Barry took a big piece of frybread and popped it into his mouth. Chewing it he said: "Not bad, not bad at all. I'm getting used to this Presidency thing."

"It's gonna take some gettin' used to son," Auntie Zeta said. "I remember when I was in my 20's and I signed up to be on the tribal school board. Not only was I elected to the board but then they named me President of the damn thing.

"People on the board wouldn't leave me alone. They would interrupt me at home when I was feeding my little family, they would stop me at the tribal center and ask me questions, hell, I couldn't take a dump without a woman crawling into the outhouse to ask me a question."

Barry's eyes got big and he decided to just thank his auntie-mom for the advice.

They each dove into their plates of food and enjoyed the rest of the night. Barry, for as grateful as he was to have his family around him, knew that he was in for a long haul and hoped that he didn't get too overwhelmed.

A few days later, over 1,000 people paid respect to the late-John Dungberry and as the last words were said at the cemetery, his widow Martha shedding her last tears over the casket, everyone that was present at the funeral turned around and left the area.

"Is that it?" Auntie Z asked Barry.

"What?" Barry whispered back.

"They all just get up and walk away from the body?" She clarified. "I mean, how come they don't watch the body get buried son?"

"That's just how they do things auntie," Barry said grabbing her hand. "I know, it's a bit different huh?"

"Different? I would say ludicrous," she said taking her hand back. "Hey kids, go over there and help those gravediggers with placing that poor old man's body in the ground!"

Barry's cousins followed her directive and they each grabbed a shovel. They started digging into the dirt when the secret service agents came over and intervened.

Barry looked over there and decided to get between the secret service and his cousins.

"Hey! Hey!" Barry exclaimed. "They mean well, guys, they are not here to hurt anyone." Barry stopped the secret service from arresting his cousins. He turned to them: "Please put the shovels down, they have men that will do this for Martha."

Reluctantly, they put the shovels down and sat down by Auntie Z. Eventually, they all piled into a van and were shuttled back to the White House.

Chapter 6: Turning the White House Red

Barry woke up the next morning and got ready for the day. It was 7 AM and he was decked out in his three-piece-suit which included his signature Tulalip logo'd bolo tie.

Over the past few days, tribal members from all over the Nation had been sending him letters, email and gifts. One of the gifts he received came from a Navajo elder who sent him a bolo tie with the US colors, representing the flag.

As he came out of his bedroom, his entire family, all nine of them were sitting in the commons area. He couldn't believe they were all there this early in the morning.

"What's going on, is there a breakfast bingo session going on?" he joked.

"No Mr. President, we're all packed and ready to go home, back to the Rez," Deb said, smiling ear-to-ear. "We're so proud of you cuz and happy for you."

Barry could see that tears were building up in her eyes and looked over her shoulder to the other family members, many of which were also crying tears of joy.

He half-hugged Deb and walked over to the rest of them who were sitting on the couches.

"You all don't have to leave now do you?" Barry asked.

Gary stood up from his seated position on the arm of the couch, pointed at Auntie Zeta and said: "Yup, we need to be hittin' the road; Auntie's got a doctor's appointment for her cataracts in a few days and we don't want to miss that."

Gary reached his hand out to shake Barry's hand; even Gary had a wisp of water in his eyes. They embraced and tears began to build in Barry's eyes.

Barry made one last attempt to pursued them from leaving: "We've got the best doctors here in the White House who can take you on as a patient Auntie?

"I mean, c'mon guys, you just got here. Besides, you owe me $20 bucks Tammie...I mean, you have all kinds of things you can do here in DC and while I'm doing my thing.."

The normally quiet, reserved Auntie Zeta stood up quickly, probably the quickest she'd ever stood up in quite some time: "Now, you listen here nephew..."

Barry stopped talking and gave her his undivided attention.

"...There's no words, NONE, that could articulate what I'm trying to tell you right now..." a smile replaced the stern look she was giving him at the beginning of her talk.

"...Grand Nephew, Barry...Mr. President, come here," she said.

Barry slowly walked up to his grand aunt and stood right in front of her so that she could see him completely. She focused her eyes on him as he approached and put her arms on his shoulders and looked up at him as she began to speak:

"Our prayers have been answered son. You are here for a reason. Nothing, no one was going to stop this from happening and now it is YOUR responsibility to use your best judgement, the beliefs, the teachings that WE gave you (she pointed at Uncle Jack and Auntie Georgianna) to the best of your ability!"

Tears began to stream down her cheeks, which made Barry begin to cry. Barry's tears made Deb cry and soon the entire 10 of them were blubbering.

Barry began to smile through the tears. He nodded and said: "Okay, okay..well, c'mon you guys, bring it in!" The other eight of them crept into Barry's and Zeta's comfort circle and they had a group hug.

Barry could see flashes of light bulbs soaking up the room as the group hug was happening. Startled, he looked up and could see a young woman in the corner of the room taking pictures of the solemn moment.

One by one, the family members gave Barry a hug and encouraging words. He watched his cousins help the elders out of the room and walk towards the front of the White House so they could get into the van and go home.

Soon, it was just Barry and the unknown photographer in the room.

"Hi, I'm Carla, your photographer," said a very attractive, Caucasian, sandy blonde hair woman who was wearing a backwards baseball cap, vest and jeans.

Wiping off the remnants of tears in the corners of his eyes, he wiped his hand off on his suit and shook her hand.

"Why are you here?" Barry asked.

"Oh, well, Dena and a few others on your team thought it would be great to have a photographer follow you around for your first week on the job," Carla replied.

"Oh really? And they sent you?" Barry said smiling.

"Yeah, I guess I was the only one available," Carla returned the smile. "Tough time to see your family go huh?"

Nodding and looking down, Barry said yes. "But, they couldn't stay here forever, so they had to go."

The two of them talked for about 20 minutes, Carla asking Barry several questions and for the most part Barry had no clue what was in store for him and by the end of the conversation, he chalked most of this experience up by saying 'it was for a reason.'

On his way to the Oval Office, he was stopped in the main hallway by a few of the team members. They were asking for signatures for some checks that needed to be given to some of the grounds crew.

As he was signing the check, he could hear some traditional hand drum singing in the distance. Could this be a sign? Could the ancestors be sending him a signal that would make him realize that he was indeed there for a reason? How lucky would he be to hear the 'old ones' communicate in this way.

Just as a buildup of excitement, gratitude and love enveloped him, he looked over to the right and there was his family members, waiting outside the women's restroom where Auntie Georgianna was singing a traditional song to help relieve herself.

He gave them the Indian nod and went about his way towards the Oval Office. He shook his head and smiled really big as he walked through the hallways.

As he approached the Oval Office, he could hear someone crying in the next room. He stopped, pointed his finger at Dena as if to say, 'One minute..' and went into the next room.

He noticed a young woman in her late 20's sitting on a couch crying. He stopped at the door and slowly went in.

"Is there something that I can help with?" Barry asked the woman who was slouched over on the couch with her hands in her face.

She looked up and with mascara running down both eyes she noticed it was the President of the United States and sat straight up.

"Uh,...(now searching for a hanky)..no, Mr. President, everything is alright," the young woman said.

Barry reached into his suit jacket and pulled out a small packet of white tissue. His late mother always told Barry to have hankies on hand as living in the Pacific Northwest, you never know when a rainstorm would come, pollen would arise or a sad movie would come on the TV and make him blubber.

"Here you go, Miss?" Barry asked.

"Oh, yeah, my name is Jonie Rudolph, I'm one of the assistants here...well, WAS one of the assistants here in the Oval Office," she said.

"WAS?" asked Barry.

"Yes, I was just let go this morning," she said sniffling.

"By who?" he asked, sitting next to her.

"Dena, sir," she said wiping her tear out of her left eye, smearing more of the mascara. "She told me that I was not cut out to be an assistant here."

"Well, I will meet with Miss Dena later today about this okay Jonie?" Barry assured her. "Now go down to the team member area and get yourself some water and we'll be in touch."

She took a deep breath and stood up. Once she stood up, Barry stood up as well and reach out to give her a handshake.

"This is all I ever wanted to do with my life, was to serve the President of the United States. I've always had the utmost respect for all of our Presidents and when the late-John was elected, I knew that it was meant to be for me to be here. I am so happy that you are President, even though it came at the expense of…well…." Jonie began to stutter her words.

Smiling, Barry said: "I know what you mean, may God rest John's soul. Now, go downstairs and take care of yourself okay?"

She nodded and began to blow her nose really loudly as she exited the room. Barry took a deep breath and exited the room after her, smiling.

He entered the Oval Office: "Sorry about that everyone, had to take care of some other business. Now, what is this meeting about?"

The door closed and Barry had a six-hour day, with meeting-after-meeting until 5 PM when he finally began to feel hungry.

"Dena, before our next meeting, please get me something from the kitchen?" Barry asked. "I'm starting to feel hungry."

Dena picked up the phone and called down to the kitchen and ordered something to eat for Barry.

It was now 8 PM and Barry was dog-tired. He stood up from his desk and put on his suit jacket. He slowly made his way from the Oval Office towards his room. Most of the team members were gone, having left to go home.

He was so tired that he didn't quite know how to think anymore. His head throbbed, his eyes were bloodshot and he could literally fall asleep on any of the nice couches that were strategically placed around the White House.

"This place is way too big!" he exclaimed as he let out a huge yawn.

"I know what you mean sir!" exclaimed a man down at the other end of the hallway.

"Who is that?" Barry asked.

"Jason, but they call me "Buzzsaw" sir," Buzzsaw said.

Barry walked closer to the man and could see he was apart of the custodial team.

"Oh, you are one of the custodians here, you help clean up the joint?" Barry said as a statement more than a question.

"Yeah, been here for quite some time," Buzzsaw said.

"How many Presidents have you been here for?" Barry asked.

"Oh, three, maybe four; well if you include Dungberry, then you'd be the fifth one sir," Buzzsaw said. "But you're right, this place is HUGE!"

"How long does it take to clean this place?" Barry asked.

"With the shit that goes on in each room, the shit in the bathrooms, the shit that we have to put up with..."

Barry interrupted him: "Man, that's a lot of shit!"

"Yeah!" Buzzsaw exclaimed. "You can just call us the shit cleaners!"

Yawning, Barry said: "Yup, you can call me the Executive President of the shit storms!"

"I don't envy the work you have to do, sir. I bet we have the same amount of shit that we have to clean up," Buzzsaw said, empathizing with Barry.

"Yeah, but I signed up for this, no one is putting a gun to my head, right?" Barry said.

"Me too, I guess. Well, I better hop to it, got more shit to clean; haven't been in the Oval yet, I'm sure there's a ton of shit in there!" Buzzsaw said smiling, pushing his cleaning cart away from Barry.

Barry kept on walking towards his room and something dawned on him as he was walking. "This place IS too big, I think I'll work on that tomorrow."

He fell asleep as soon as his head hit the pillow.

The next morning, he woke up very excited. His goal for the day wasn't to figure out how to eliminate the US Deficit, how to keep peace in the Middle East, but to figure out where he could live where he didn't need a map to know where each room was located.

It was now 9 AM and Ursula Tally, US Press Secretary and Dena Montana, Executive Assistant were hustling down the hallways of the White House.

"Anyone see the President?" Ursula hollered out.

"Have you seen Mr. Whiteman?" Dena screamed out.

Barry had on corduroy overalls, a white under t-shirt, workman's boots and red bandana around his head as he was using duct tape to keep people from going in or out of one wing of the White House.

"Mr. Whiteman!!" Ursula exclaimed.

Smiling big and stretching the grey duct tape from the roll, Barry said: "Yes? How may I help you?"

"What are you doing Mr. President?" asked Ursula.

"Oh, nothing, just making the White House smaller," Barry said and used his teeth to rip the long piece of tape that he just stretched out.

Barry had already used four rolls of duct tape to create a spider's web so that no one could go in or out.

"Don't you think that someone else could have done that for you?" Ursula asked and Dena nodding her head in agreement.

"Nope," he said stretching another piece of tape out from the roll. "Next, is that other wing over there," Barry used his thick Tulalip lips to point at the staircase adjacent to the wing they were standing.

"Not the third floor!" cried Ursula. "That leads to the White House Solarium, Game Room, Linen Room, a Diet Kitchen, and another sitting room which was previously used as President George W. Bush's workout room."

"Exactly!" Barry exclaimed. "What Indian needs all that space? Can you imagine the electricity bill? The heating bill itself must be in the thousands of dollars a month just for that space. Nah, I don't need it. We'll save the taxpayers a ton of money by getting rid of those rooms."

"Uh,...uh..." Ursula didn't know what to say. "Okay?"

Ursula knew that it sounded good and when the Press got their hands on this information, they would have a field day.

"Well, you have a press conference in 20 minutes Mr. President," Ursula said. "Will you be ready in time?"

"Heck yeah, I'll go like this," Barry said, pointing to his get up.

"Are you sure Mr. Whiteman?" Dena asked.

"Why, what's wrong with what I have on?" Barry asked. "The overalls were a gift from my Auntie Zeta. My boots were worn by my late father and..."

"We get the hint," Ursula said. "Okay, we'll be in the Press Room when you want to come in. Here are your notes and yes, we'll get the teleprompter ready."

About 15 minutes later, an underdressed President Whitman showed up to the Press Room. Immediately shutters on cameras started a flood of noise and white flash bulbs filled the room as the President went behind the podium.

"Doing some renovations to the White House sir?" asked one reporter in the front row.

"Already making changes eh?!" said another one.

"Painting a new picture sir?!" a female reporter yelled out.

"Now, now..everyone please hold your questions to the end of this talk," Barry directed them.

"You know, as a young boy, growing up on the Tulalip reservation, we grew up in very modest ...and I mean, modest..hell, I'll just say it. We grew up very poor and we had to make due with what we had.

"We grew up in a small HUD home.."

A small Jewish reporter whispered to his colleague: "HUD?"

"Housing of Urban Development," whispered the other reporter in response.

"....we didn't have food sometimes and we didn't have heat sometimes," Barry continued. "I'm very proud of my late parents for making the most of what we did have and allowing us to make ends-meet.

"Just like Tupac said in that song 'Mama', "you made miracles every Thanksgiving"..yup, that was my parents. To this day, I don't know how the hell they got us through the really tough times.

"So, now that my new residence is The White House, I have decided to make some changes to the layout of the place so that I don't need to ask Siri where this or that room is located."

"What does that mean sir?" the small Jewish reporter shouted.

"It means that I have eliminated the use of the third floor and above so that (a), I don't need to know where to get lost (b) it will shrink the place down considerably since it's just me that lives there and (c) it will reduce the energy output needed to make the White House go, which will reduce taxpayer dollars needed to fund the place," Barry announced.

The first time in White House press conference history, 'The Press' gave the President a resounding round of applause.

"Now..now...I'm just doing my part to reduce the deficit this country is in; which is the real reason why you were all called to this event," Barry said.

"Oh, before I get to the bullet points for this press conference, I need to tell you that I am reserving one of the guest bedrooms near my room for my two pets that will be coming to stay with me.

"Chummy and Daisy will be staying with me starting next week. Chummy is my dog; a mutt or a mixture of different types of dog. Daisy is my pet salmon whom I have had for 20 years,...okay, now to the business at hand."

Chapter 7: WTF?!

Donald Duckson and Sherry Montgomery were sitting in their usual spots at the bar when the TV at the bar went from commercial to 'Breaking News.'

"Breaking news tonight as President Whiteman, dressed in overalls and boots came out to address the media," said Janice Thompson, CNN Host. "We'll bring in David Satler and James Blufield who have been helping us sort through our political news; David, what do you make of what the President is wearing?"

"Whatever he is doing, he is making a mockery of the entire Presidential system," Satler said.

"I agree," Blufield chimed in. "I mean, taping off the third floor to save taxpayer's money? What does that all really mean?"

"He got a round of applause from those who were present at the press conference," Thompson said.

"Yeah, but so what? I remember when President Bush number 2 got a round of applause from the press when he announced he was going for a jog around the White House," Blufield said.

Meanwhile, at the The Spot bar, Sherry and Donald were there watching CNN's broadcast.

"What the hell is going on?" Sherry said, as she took a shot of tequila. Slamming the shot glass on the bar top, she exclaimed: "Why the hell is HE our President?"

"There there now, in due time,...in duuuue time," Duckson said as he sipped on his dark beer.

"In other news from that press conference," Thompson said, "Here are some footage of the President's new pets, a dog, whom the President calls 'Chummy' and a King Salmon, whom the President calls 'Daisy' are the newest residents in the White House."

"That's got to be the ugliest looking dog I've ever did see," Sherry said. "I mean look at it, it doesn't even move when the cameramen are standing right by it. Is it breathing?"

"A King salmon for a pet?" Blufield said. "I've never seen such a thing in any walk of life. Aren't salmon an endangered species?"

"Not yet," said Satler. "If the President's tribe and others are out there overharvesting, they may storm the White House in search of that salmon sitting in that tank."

It has now been a month since the swearing-in as President and Barry's handlers have advised him that he needs to start thinking of naming a vice president.

So, they set up a dinner meeting of five candidates: three women and two men that Barry could engage with at a sit-down dinner.

The dinner would be served on the same floor (one of two open floors) as the President's and the two pet's rooms.

All five candidates came into the dining room at the same time and Barry gave each one of them a different type of handshake or 'daps' as the young street kids call it.

They each sat down and placed their napkins on their laps. Barry, sitting at the head of the table, welcomed them to the dinner.

Wearing a nice blue tuxedo and his customary Tulalip Tribes bolo tie.

"I'd like to welcome you all here to the White House," Barry said with a big smile on his face. "I'm sure you've noticed many of the (puts up air quotes) renovations that I've done the past few days.

"You're gathered here tonight to allow me to gauge our level of interest in you as a possible replacement of myself as the Vice President of the United States."

Barry looked down and got a bit sentimental: "The untimely death of John thrusted me into this current position of President. I've learned quite a bit these first 30 days in office and am still learning as I go.

"My elders once taught me that you never stop learning. They molded me, mostly slapping me on the back of the head until I learned, but nonetheless, they molded me into the man that you see today.

"I'm not going to mold any one of you, in fact, I want you to be creative. I want you to be yourselves and I want you to be able to act on behalf of the United States in a professional, and yes, loving manner."

Just as Barry was going to go into another part of his talk, the servers came out with the first course; a plate of Caesar salad.

Each person, while still listening to Barry, began to stab their pieces of lettuce, covered in Caesar salad dressing and freshly shredded cheese.

"So, here you all are, each handpicked by me and my team. I want to get to know each of you tonight and engage in a few questions that will or better yet, should, spark your interest," Barry said.

"Excuse me, if I may," said George Hamilton, Hawaii Governor and the gentleman sitting to Barry's left. "How were we all chosen?"

"Good question Mr. Hamilton," Barry said.

"George, please..call me George," he said smiling big and even gloating a bit at the other participants.

"Okay, Mr. George, you were all handpicked because you represent an underprivileged section of our wonderful country.

"Yvonne Underwood," Barry said as Yvonne stopped chewing gave Barry her undivided attention. "You were chosen because of your work with the women of the great state of Texas. As Governor, you have done an amazing job of helping raise wages for women; you've fought hard for funding women's shelters across Texas. Congratulations on the fine work you've done.

"Ivan Rappaport," Barry said, pointing fully across the table with his lips. "You've done a great job with our youth in the great state of Florida. In a state that is known for retirees, you've done an amazing job of helping with prevention programs and have done wonderful things in the school systems.

"Harry Ostreiler, as State Representative of my home state of Washington, you've done an amazing job with the GLBT community," Barry said, lifting up his glass of water to 'cheers' him. "Congratulations on fighting for our gay and lesbian, transgenders; it's not an easy battle, but you've done it with style and grace.

"Eva Mentes, as Chief Financial Officer of a Fortune 500 company, your work in the financial advising community for the impoverished of the Northeast section of our country has been thoroughly documented and it hasn't gone unnoticed. Well done young lady!

"Finally, Mr. George Hamilton," Barry said, looking to his left. "Honestly, I don't know why you are here and you are now excused."

"Excused?" George awkwardly asked.

"Yes, Mr. George, excused," Barry replied. "I'm not sure how or why you were invited here, your comments against the late John have also been well documented and I am sure whomever on my team recommended you to come to this dinner will be released as well. Good night sir."

George put his fork down and pushed himself away from the table. His face was now blushing red and beads of sweat formed on his big forehead.

"Ladies?" George said as he excused himself from the table and began to walk towards the exit.

"Oh, and Mr. George?" Barry stopped George from leaving.

George turned around and did not verbally respond.

"This dinner that you're at is highly confidential. Things that I have said thus far are forbidden to be told outside of these walls, do you understand me?" Barry asked.

George bowed half way forward as if to say, 'your wish is my command.' He turned around and exited the room.

At the dinner table, the rest of the four participants each sat up more straight at their seat and gave Barry their undivided attention.

"I'm sorry that you had to witness that you guys," Barry said. "That was done on purpose. IF we get to work together, you'll see that I got to this seat, not by happenstance like the media is portraying, but because I am savvy and I understand how this whole political thing works."

For the next two hours, and as each course of food came out, Barry asked them all some intriguing questions about the state of the union, the political issues around law enforcement, ..you know, important questions like who was going to win the Superbowl.

After dessert was finished and dessert wine was polished off, each of them stood up and began to walk towards the exit of the dining room.

The President, standing by the exit, shook each of their hands with the two women almost competing with how they said good night. Eva started with a handshake but then gave him a hug. Yvonne seeing that Eva gave him a hug, decided to kiss the President on the cheek. Eva saw that and began to kiss the President on the lips; a peck, and as Yvonne was about to make out with the President, Barry stepped backwards and waved at all five of them and retreated back to his bedroom.

The next morning, the President was updating his team and the topic of choosing the next Vice President was next on the agenda.

"After wining and dining with some of the most intriguing people of our Country, I am going to recommend who should be our next Vice President.

"I'll first tell you who the four candidates were," Barry said outlining all four of them to the team. "Next, I'll tell you who I am not going to recommend.

"As much as I love the women that you helped me handpick, at the end of the night, it got a bit 'hot under the collar' and I don't think I can work with either of them.

"Therefore, it's down to the two gentlemen, Harry and Ivan. Although Ivan comes from a great state and he's done wonders with our youth, I'm going to recommend we go with Harry.

"Harry has worked with our Gay and Lesbian community, which for one, has a great track record for voting and should help us in the next election. Secondly, he comes from Washington State as well and we've worked together a few times while I was chair of my tribe.

"So, Lucy, David and Tom, make sure that we keep Harry here with us for a few days while we negotiate his stay and release the other three. Get them each a parting gift for coming in 2nd, 3rd and 4th place," Barry instructed.

"What should we give them sir?" Tom asked.

"I dunno, something really special," Barry said. "Oh, I know, get them one of them fancy slow cookers. Mama always used a slow cooker to make pot roast. Gosh, I miss my mama's cooking. Yup, the slow cooker it is."

Tom wrote that down on his pad of paper and the three of the team members left the Oval Office to do as the President requested.

"Dena! What's next on the day's agenda?" Barry shouted in Dena's direction. She was sitting on the couch next to the exit of the Oval Office.

"Uh, it looks like you have a run? Are you going for a jog this morning sir?" Dena asked.

"Oh! Yes, thanks for reminding me. I gotta get moving and get my runners on," Barry said standing straight up and making his way towards the hallway.

10 minutes later, Barry was ready for his run. He had on typical rez workout gear, you know, the red bandana, sun glasses, the hoodie sweater that was a size too big, the spandex pants and his Nike shoes.

"C'mon Chummy!" Barry exclaimed and whistled loudly to get his dog's attention. Barry began to run in place while he waited for Chummy to come over to him. He stopped and looked over at where Chummy was laying down. Chummy was still laying down, he only glanced up at Barry when Barry whistled at him.

"C'mon you dumb dog! Let's go for a run!" Barry exclaimed and slapped his hand on his own thigh trying to will his dog over to him like a Jedi knight.

A secret serviceman went over and tried to lift Chummy up on his four legs and Chummy responded with a huge growl, exposing his front teeth. The secret serviceman hopped back and looked at his supervisor and shrugged his shoulders.

"Ah, I know what Chummy needs. Hey Dena, did we get Chummy his coffee for the morning?" Barry asked.

"Coffee? Sir?" Dena asked.

"Yes, didn't I specifically tell you that he needs his morning coffee?" Barry asked.

"Yes, you did sir and yes we did give him some," Dena said pointing at the food bowl next to where Chummy was lying.

Barry went over to the bowl and took a sip. "Nope, this is not dark enough coffee. I told you Dena, he needs dark, dark, almost muddy coffee to wake up. That's what we call on the reservation some fisherman's coffee."

Dena picked up her cell phone and called down to the kitchen and ordered a new batch of coffee to be made, 'extra muddy'.

"Well, we don't have time to wait, we gotta hit the road. Next time Chummy!" Barry exclaimed as he bolted out of the White House front doors and out onto the secured path that the secret service made for him.

Later that day, CNN reported another "Breaking News" story about Barry taking his first jog as The President.

"As you can see here, the wardrobe that was given to The President is a bit controversial. I mean we're getting a lot of phone calls from peace activists around the United States questioning the President's use of the red bandana," said Wolfe Blitzer.

"We'll bring in Janice Thompson who is on the streets of New York this afternoon as she is asking local New York residents what they think of the President's use of a red bandana; Janice?" Blitzer turned the attention to her.

"Yes, Wolfe, I am downtown at New York's Times Square and I have with me Mrs. Dawnell Williams, a mother of four. Mrs.

Williams, you are clearly African American and how does it strike you that the President is wearing a red bandana?"

"I despise it. Who does he think he is wearing that thing? I mean, as a mother of four, who is raising the future of our country, I do whatever I can to keep the gangs and the violence away from my children!" Williams said.

"Do you think this is racially motivated, I mean, the President is Native American and I don't think there are too many gangs on reservations around the Country?" Janice asked Williams.

"The bandana is red, that's all that matters. Doesn't he make enough money to get himself a bandana that isn't red or blue?" Williams asked.

"There you have it Wolfe, the bandana needs to go! Back to you in the studios," Janice kicked the story back to Wolfe Blitzer in the CNN studios.

The newspapers, the magazines, emails and websites all dubbed Barry as the Gangster President. This would be something that Ursula and her team of public relations/press relations experts would have to spin around to make it not so bad, going forward.

Chapter 8: The Spin Cycle

"Our next guest, comes from the great Pacific Northwest. He is our first Native American President and needs no real introduction..well, wait he does, who is this guy? Let's bring him out, the Chief, the leader of the free world, yours and my President, President Barry Whiteman!" Jimmy Kimmel introduced Barry and Barry came out wearing his red bandana, his blue suit, and customary Tulalip Tribes beaded bolo tie.

He waved his hand and took off the bandana and waved in the air. The background music was not the normal popular song that most guests get when they came out, but instead it was a group of bird singers that came over from San Manual Tribe near Riverside, CA.

Barry stopped in his path towards the stage where Jimmy was standing and did a little Bird Song dance, stopped, stuck his tongue out and smiled really big. He waved again and went over to Jimmy and shook his hand.

Jimmy Kimmel pulled Barry closer to him and gave him a hug. He whispered something into his ear: "When Dove's Cry."

That comment made Barry uncomfortable for a minute and he looked into Jimmy's eyes with a massive look of confusion.

"Go ahead Mr. President, have a seat right there on the couch," Jimmy pointed at the blue couch next to the desk on stage.

Barry turned around and waved at the crowd and took a seat. He unbuckled his suit jacket and got comfortable.

"Wow, look at the way you're sitting Mr. President, you're not sitting in a Chief position, like we were all taught in pre-school," Jimmy said.

"No, no, I moved past Chief position back in high school, barely! Just barely!" Barry said.

"So, how is it, Mr. President, coming from the reservation and now becoming the leader of the free world?" Jimmy asked as a round of applause echoed throughout the studio.

"No, no, it was nothing...really," Barry said smiling. "I mean, I want to thank Donald Duckson and Sherry Montgomery for their role in my Presidency."

Oooooohs and aaaahhhhs came from the capacity crowd.

"Now, now, I mean that with all sincerity. They ran a good hard race, but in the end they are both at home doing good things for their communities and I am here with you," Barry said.

"Well you did make a reservation to be here, sir," Jimmy said smiling.

"Yes, yes I did but you're the one who accepted me just like the late John did, may God rest his soul," Barry said looking down.

"What do you think the late-John is saying about you now up in Heaven?" Jimmy asked.

"John? Oh, he's probably looking down at me right now saying, (in a strong southern twang) Barry..don't you go messin' this thing up now, do us proud!"

The crowd started to clap in appreciation for the late John Dungberry.

"I want to extend my love and appreciation to John's widow Martha for sharing John with us and the world!" Barry said.

The crowd began to clap again and a tear started to form in Barry's left eye. Jimmy saw that and said:

"Now, now, Mr. President, nothing to get all choked up about."

Boos started to echo in the studio.

"What? Too early for that?" Jimmy said shrugging his shoulders. "Okay, let's get into some real talk here, now I know that you have taken some heat for wearing that red bandana. Mr. President, why red? You could've chosen any color of the rainbow to use, heck, I heard you're a big Seahawks fan, why not use a Seahawks bandana?"

"Well, Jimmy, you ever have a habit?" Barry asked.

"None that I want to talk about over the airwaves with you about!" Jimmy exclaimed.

"Well, I have a habit of doing the same things that got you to where you want to go. Wearing this red bandana is something I've been doing since the late 80's. As a young man, growing up on the rez, I got this red bandana from my late grandfather.

"He wore this same red bandana when he would go reef net fishing on Tulalip Bay," Barry said as he handed Jimmy the bandana.

"This is the same bandana that your late grandfather wore?" Jimmy questioned looking down at the bandana and now holding it with his first finger and thumb.

"Yes Jimmy, that's the same one. And I'm sorry that if someone thinks that since I wore it, I am now a gang banger or excuse me, a person who values illegal gangs," Barry explained.

"So, you're not in a gang?" Jimmy said jokingly, although when Jimmy speaks, you don't quite know if he's joking or not.

"No, Jimmy, I'm not in a gang. I don't condone gangs, I don't believe in violence and in fact, this has sparked us to do something about the gang violence," Barry said.

"Oh, you're going to make it a law that you can't be in a gang? Mr. President, that would be so fabulous, all of us who live in the greater Los Angeles and New York areas would just love you for that!" Jimmy exclaimed.

"No, Jimmy, I'm sorry, but I can't do that because of our Constitution and Bill of Rights; however, what I plan to do, is to start a new campaign called 'Take Back What's Ours' campaign; an anti-drug movement that will hopefully educate those who believe that selling drugs or ingesting drugs is a good thing; that it really isn't a good thing," Barry said.

Round of applause again throughout the audience.

"Valiant, very valiant Mr. President," Jimmy said, half clapping as he talked. "Well, we know you're a busy man so we'll let you go. The President of the United States!"

Barry stood up and waved at the audience and as he gave Jimmy another handshake-hug, Jimmy whispered in his ear again: "You got the look."

Barry again gave him that side, confused look that our elders gave us when we tried to tell them they are wrong about something they just said.

As Barry was getting into the limousine, he yelled out at Dena: "Talk to Jimmy's guys and ask him what it means when he told me: 'When dove's cry and You got the look.'"

"Those are the late Prince's songs sir," Dena said as she was writing down the names of the songs on her notepad.

"I know that Dena, but why did Jimmy whisper those things in my ear?" Barry asked as he unbuckled his bolo tie and got a bit more comfortable.

The next day, Barry was about to go out onto the West Lawn of the White House to give a speech about the new campaign that he announced in Los Angeles while on the Jimmy Kimmel Show.

"Okay, Mr. President, the media is ready for you," said a White House assistant to the Press Secretary. The doors opened and he slowly walked to the podium.

A batch of reporters were lined up waiting for him to speak. A 2'x4' banner was taped up to the front of the podium with the campaign slogan: 'Take Back What's Ours'.

As he was talking, US residents all around the world who were watching him live on TV, at their desks while working or on their cell phones using Twitter, saw the President talking and the campaign slogan in plain sight.

"What the hell is he talking about now?" said one resident.

"Does he really think we're giving him back the land that they think they are owed?" said another US resident.

Twitter, Facebook, and all social media started to light up with comments, mostly negative ones about the new campaign slogan.

Duckson's phone rang and on the other end was Sherry: "Are you watching this?"

Duckson who was at his home was brushing the fur on his poodle, whom he thought was going to be the 'first dog' when he received him earlier in the year.

"Yup, I am on it!" Duckson replied.

"Take Back What's Ours! Brilliant Mr. President, simply brilliant!" Sherry said.

"How do we spin this?" Duckson said as he had his cell in between his right shoulder and his ear so that he could be 'hands free' in brushing his dog.

"Easy. We call our friends, our land conservationists, as well as the right wingers who feel that this land was always non-Indians land and get them to start exercising their First Amendment rights," Sherry said. "We'll just keep pecking at him Donald, and he'll buckle...oh yes, he'll buckle."

It had been two weeks since the new campaign "Take Back What's Ours" began and new poll numbers came out.

"Breaking News today as new Gallup Poll numbers show the President's approval rating has dipped significantly," Wolfe Blitzer reported.

"A month ago, the President was at a whopping 72% approval rating and as of this morning, he's down to 42%. We'll bring in our two political advisors, David Satler and James Blufield to discuss these shocking numbers.

"David, what do you attribute the 30-point decline in the President's approval rating?" Wolfe asked Satler.

"The new campaign, plain and simple. It's not resonating with the American public," Satler said.

"Why would it?" Blufield interjected. "I mean here you have a Native American President, who looks Native American with the long hair, the beaded necklace for a tie, the whole gettup saying Take-Back-What's-Ours..what was he thinking?"

"All anti-Whiteman supporters are licking their chops at this news Wolfe. It's been a complete disaster!" Satler said.

"How do you turn the numbers around, if you are in the Oval Office this afternoon?" Wolfe asked.

"You change that damn slogan, that's what you do," Blufield said.

"Punt, Wolfe. You punt on this whole idea and start from scratch," Satler said.

"Yup, the President and his team will have some serious soul searching to do. In other news today, ..." Wolfe went onto another story.

Meanwhile, back in the Oval Office, the President had his entire team sitting waiting for his arrival for an emergency meeting.

The door opened and a secret serviceman held it open as Barry walked in. The entire team stood up as the President walked in.

"Really you guys? You really don't have to stand up when I walk into the room,...please have a seat," Barry said as he took off his suit jacket.

They all sat down and Barry began to speak: "I'm not like the other Presidents that you either worked for or heard about. In fact, why I signed up to be the Vice President was because the late-John said we would act differently than the other ones that have ever sat in this seat.

"I wanted and still want to do things differently than Barack, George I and II, John and Abraham. I want to make changes that will only help our people, ALL people.

"So, numbers of approval ratings don't really upset me, but what does upset me the most is that the work we're doing is not resonating with the lamens American.

"Our goal, when we set foot to start this campaign was to wrap our arms around the opioid and other illegal drug epidemic that are killing Americans.

"Just the other day, we laid to rest a young Tulalip kid, only 15-years-old who was shooting up heroin and because it had Fentanyl, the same drug that killed Prince and Michael Jackson!" Barry said.

"I don't mean to bring you all down, but we need to do something to stop this. Our latest campaign, although well-intended to stop Americans from doing drugs, is being heavily criticized because our opponents are spinning it in their direction.

"As I've said, I am humble enough to not care about my personal approval ratings of Joe Voter, what I do care about is making actual change and saving people's lives.

"Are you in with me?!" Barry asked the group.

"YES!" they all said in unison.

"Can we make positive change?" Barry asked again.

"YES!" they said.

"Can we save lives?!" Barry exclaimed as he got on top of the desk in the Oval Office.

"YES!!" They all said with one fist in the air.

"Now let's get to work!!" Barry said and hopped off the desk and shook hands with each of them as they energetically left the Oval Office.

The next day, Barry asked Dena to get Ursula and Carla in the Oval Office immediately.

"Uh, sir, are you okay?" Dena asked nervously.

"What do you mean am I okay Dena, just do as I ask!" shouted Barry through the intercom.

Ten minutes later, Ursula knocked at the door.

"Come in," Barry said as he put down a newspaper that he was reading.

Carla was right behind Ursula, almost using Carla as a shield.

"Is everything okay sir?" Ursula asked.

"Okay?! Okay?! What's the meaning of this?" Barry asked as he held up the Washington Post newspaper which showed Barry addressing his team from yesterday's meeting.

"It looks like you are on the front page of the paper sir," she said.

"Who told you to put me on the front page of the paper? Actually, who asked you (pointing at Carla) to take pictures of me during a private meeting with my team?" Barry interrogated them.

"Uh..uh," Ursula stammered.

"I just came in on my own, sir, Ursula had nothing to do with that," Carla said.

"You did huh?" Barry asked Carla. She nodded yes. Barry looked at Ursula who agreed with Carla.

"Well that's too bad Ursula," Barry said shaking his head in disappointment.

"Too bad sir?" Ursula asked.

"Yup, too bad because I was going to commend you for the fine work, young lady!" Barry said as he flashed a smile.

"Fine work, sir?" Ursula's body language changed from being a battered housewife to being a superhero.

"Yes! This is fine work! Risky, but excellent work. And that camera angle, Carla, I didn't even know you were in the room!" Barry exclaimed.

"I used my 'Go Pro' Mr. President and yup, it was supposed to catch you when you didn't know it was coming. It comes out more authentically that way," Carla said with a proud look on her face.

"Come here and look at the posts that are online underneath the picture and headline," Barry said waving both of them behind his chair so that they could scroll down and see the hundreds of positive comments.

"Momentum is ours ladies, now let's go and make it happen!"

Chapter 10: Getting Defensive

A knock at the door of the Oval Office and Dena's head poked inside.

"Sir, you have a moment for Damon Rasmussen, National Security Advisor?"

"Yes, please bring him in," Barry said as he through down a packet of information he received that morning.

Rasmussen, all 6'5" of him marched into the Oval Office. Barry invited him to have a seat on the couch and he plopped himself down on the adjacent couch.

"What may I do you for?" Barry asked.

"Well Mr. President, we have an issue," Rasmussen said. "I know that we're on an anti-drug campaign and we're all for it in the Pentagon.

"What's the end game for ending the war on terror? What do we want from the Middle East?" Rasmussen asked.

"Well, ..well…" The President didn't know. He had no clue what to say to the National Security Advisor.

"Well what sir?" Rasmussen asked.

"Suitsen Oheliq, kwenes ena tachel…" Barry started to talk in Coast Salish dialect, something he did when he didn't know the answer to something. He'd been doing that since he was in high school, it was more of a nervous tick.

When he was a Senior at Marysville Pilchuck High School he had simply adored Jenny, a Junior. She was the cat's meow, the dog's pajamas, you get the hint.

Every day, he built up the nerve to go up to her and ask her to go on a date with him. She would turn around and face him from her locker and he would say: "Jenny?"

She said: "Yes Barry?"

"Um..um…" Barry didn't know what to say. He was blinded by her beauty.

He began to talk Coast Salish to her and was asking her out in that dialect, not English.

"Excuse me? How dare you say that to me?!" she said slapping Barry in the face and walked away.

Here Barry was again, in a pickle, not knowing the answers that Rasmussen was asking. They were simple answers that an average President would know, but since he was still very much learning his new job, he didn't quite know what to say.

He began to sweat and decided to play 'dumb Indian.' Dumb Indian is an old Indian politician move that Barry learned along the way.

Anytime you hear an Indian politician ask the question on top of a question, normally that is Indian for: "I don't know the answer and I'm too proud to say I don't know. So to buy me time, I will ask a question on top of that question that you just asked me."

"Mr. President, are you with me?" Rasmussen asked.

"Huh?" Barry asked back.

"I am asking if you are focused on the questions I have asked you, sir, we really need some answers right now about the questions I have because…" Rasmussen said.

Barry interrupted: "Look, go and get Granger (the Secretary of Defense), go get Ursula and let's get the Cabinet together to answer these questions so that we're all on the same page?"

"Ursula sir? Why would we need the Press Secretary in on this meeting sir?" Rasmussen asked.

"Just do it?! Or do you want me to?" Barry asked.

"No sir, I can handle that. We want to meet in the West Wing?" Rasmussen asked.

"No, let's meet in the Chief of Staff's room just down the hall," Barry instructed.

Rasmussen turned around and exited the Oval Office.

20 minutes later, all of the ones that Barry asked for were sitting in the Chief of Staff's room.

Dena poked her head in the Oval Office. "Sir? They are all awaiting your arrival now inside the Chief of Staff's room like you requested," she said.

Barry was heavy into meditation, sitting on the edge of the seat on one of the couches with the lights turned off.

"Huh? Oh, okay, I'll be right there," he said and stood up, stretched out his neck and did a few air squats. He put on his suit jacket and placed his feet back into his shoes and headed out towards the meeting.

As he entered the room, there were several people in there that Barry didn't ask for but were there anyway; mostly staffers of the ones that he wanted in the meeting.

"Why are they here?" Barry asked, using his lips to point over to the young staffers that were sitting in a clump to the President's left.

"Oh, sir, yes, they are our team and we want them in here so that they can hear what the direction is going forward with some of these topics," Ashton Granger, the Secretary of Defense said.

"I don't want them here for this meeting, please excuse them," Barry said.

Granger looked at the young staff members and gave them the nod to leave. They got up and collected their belongings and walked out of the room.

"Okay, so it sounds like we have a lot to talk about, questions that National Security Advisor Rasmussen has for the team," Barry said, looking at Rasmussen who was sitting to Barry's right.

"Yes, thank you Mr. President, yes, we have a lot to go over and it was instructed that we all gather to talk about those issues now," Rasmussen said. "Mr. President, what is our position on the Middle East?"

Barry popped in a piece of Bubblicious, watermelon flavor, and began to chew it intently.

"Now...now...(chomp chomp chomp)...now, when you say our position, you are saying you want to know how we think about the Middle East, right?" Barry asked.

"Uh, yes sir, what do we want to do if it flares up again?" Rasmussen asked.

"Flares up? What's the matter does it have the clap?" Barry started to chuckle and used his back hand to tap Ursula on the shoulder. She blinked her eyes rapidly and took a deep breath.

"Do we need to call the Middle East a doctor?" Barry started chuckling again.

"Sir, really, we need to know your directive on this," Rasmussen said.

"Ursula, what do you think?" Barry asked as he popped in another piece of bubble gum.

Rasmussen rolled his eyes and took a deep breath.

"The Middle East? I think we should be in a wait-and-see position sir; we don't know all of the answers as the parts are always moving there," she said.

"Wait and see position, with all due respect sir, I don't agree.." Rasmussen began to make his claim.

"Hold on, hold your fussy big britches cowboy, let the woman speak," Barry said, barely able to make out the sounds of each word over the massive amounts of gum inside his mouth.

A bit of saliva escaped Barry's mouth as he began to speak. He quickly used his suit coat sleeve to wipe up the liquid, smiling he said: "Go ahead Ursula, keep reelin' that fishing rod out there."

"Well, as I was saying, we don't know all the information that is coming from over there and if we push too fast we may lose the contacts that are giving us that intel and if we wait too long, we may lose them anyway, so yes, I think we wait and see sir," Ursula said as she sat back in her chair.

"Intel, Ursula?" Barry quizzed her.

"Intel---igence, intel is short for intelligence," Ursula said.

"I know. I know. Just making sure we're on the same page. Don't want to..ya know...don't want to ...assume anything. You know assuming is short for making an ass out of you and me,..." Barry said, chomping away at his gum.

"Again, with all due respect sir, we need to take a stronger position in the Middle East," Rasmussen firmly said. "If we don't sir, we risk so much of our reputation, we'll be the laughing stock of NATO and we need to make sure we make a strong presence sir."

"You know Rasmussen," Barry said, putting his left ankle up on his right knee, "have you ever gone hunting before?"

Looking around the room as if to say, 'what does this have to do with anything?' Rasmussen said: "Sure, yes, I've been hunting a few times. I grew up in Montana where there is a lot of elk."

"Good, good..yes, then you know when you go hunting, you set up your spot, right? You first check to see what the weather is going to be like and make sure you wear proper clothing. You don't want to be stuck out there when it's cold with no thermal underwear," Barry said.

He gave Ursula a nudge with his left elbow which shook her up a little bit: "You really don't want to be out there when it starts to rain and you don't have your wet gear on..."

"Your point, sir?" Rasmussen asked.

"My point, Rasmussen, is that when we position ourselves to go after that elk, or in this case, the Middle East, we don't want to position ourselves in a place where we will scare them away. We want to be prepared. We want to know how we will react if that elk should come up a different hill or at least a hill that we didn't expect them," Barry explained.

"Where we didn't expect them sir?" Rasmussen asked.

"YES! We want to know as much details as we can because we only get one shot at the elk or in this case the Middle East," Barry said smiling nice and big. He turned around and spit out his big clump of gum towards the waste paper basket but the gum only went 2 feet from his chair.

Barry stood up and awkwardly picked up the gum from the carpet and tried to place it in the trash. The gum was already stuck to the carpet and so as he picked up the gum it produced a long string, almost like taffy being stretched out.

He snapped his wrist trying to get the gum from his fingers but it wasn't working.

"Listen, I gotta take care of this, let's adjourn until tomorrow when we can pick this up again?" Barry asked the group.

He began to walk out of the room to a bunch of murmurs around the room. He closed the door behind him and leaned up on it. He took a deep breath and went to the restroom.

Later that day as Barry was heading out of the Oval Office, Ursula stopped him in the hallway.

"Oh, sir, you gotta minute?" she asked.

"Sure, what's on your mind?" he replied.

"That whole bit in the Chief of Staff office, was that just a ploy or did you really care what I thought of the next moves we should take in the Middle East?" she asked.

Pausing for a few breaths, Barry said: "Both. Yup, it was a ploy to show the rest of the team that I am the type of leader that values all of his team member's thoughts and opinions. And, I do believe that you are very smart and didn't get to the White House for your pretty looks," he said.

"Pretty looks huh? You think I'm pretty?" she was slightly blushing as she said that.

"Oh, definitely," he replied.

"In a cute, daffodil way or a hot, red roses-type of way?" she wanted confirmation of what he meant.

"Your looks aren't as controversial as Monica Lewinski was with Bill, but it isn't as simple as Hillary's love for him neither," he explained.

"I'm confused," Ursula confessed.

"That's okay, it won't be the last time that will happen around me," he replied.

"Well, whatever you are trying to say, I'm saying thank you," Ursula said putting her hand on his shoulder.

Just as she was putting her hand up on his shoulder, Dena came walking by. She looked directly at Ursula's hand and wrist, then with big eyes, she looked at Ursula.

Ursula began to wipe away at the lint on Barry's shoulder as if to imply he had dandruff on it.

"Thank you sir, for your time, I better be....better be heading back to...(she points to the left, then to the right)...that way!" Ursula said and exited stage left.

Barry smiled, shook his head and went on his way back to retreat to his bedroom.

Chapter 11: Turbulance Abounds

As Barry walked into the Oval Office, the slender, hour-glass shaped body of Ursula had her back towards the entrance.

"Well, good morning Miss Ursula," Barry greeted her.

She quickly turned around and was a bit startled. "Good morning Mr. President, sleep well?" she asked.

"Yes, believe it or not I did," he replied smiling and nodding. "What do I owe this nice surprise this fine DC morning?"

Just as he asked that, Dena was escorting a mother and son into the Oval Office.

"Mr. President, I'd like to introduce you to Ms. Carmen Santiago and her 5-year-old son Delano," Ursula said. "Delano won a Washington Post 'Meet the President' essay contest with his piece entitled: "The President's Hair."

Ursula held up the newspaper with the essay and a hand written drawing of President Whiteman in front of what looked like the White House and a stick figure of a person with A LOT of hair.

"H…h…hi Mr. …Mr….Mr. Preth-ident," said Delano with a very strong lisp.

Barry bent down and went on one knee. "Why hello there Delano, how are you today?"

"I'm…I'm…I'm just fine today th-errr," Delano replied.

Barry grabbed the newspaper from Ursula's hand and began to read the essay.

"Wow, look at this, your essay was in the newspaper huh?" Barry asked the little man.

"Yeth..yeth it wa-th, th-errr...my mom...my mom th-ed it wa-th the be-th thing that could've happened to me," Delano said.

"Well, was it?" Barry said, glancing back at the newspaper.

"I worked really hard on it th-err and ye-th it wa-th the be-th thing that ha-th happened to me in my entire life!!" he said smiling from ear-to-ear, exposing his Jack-o-lantern grin.

"Look at here, in your essay, you wrote: "Barry Whiteman has a lot of hair. At first I thought he was a girl, but then I learned that some Native Indians have long hair," Barry said.

"Ye-th, I'm th-awee th-err if that make-th you mad that I th-ed that you looked like a girl, but I'm ju-th a little boy and I'm th-till learning about Indian-th," Delano said, looking down.

Barry stood up and reached down to give Delano a handshake.

"Your essay was well informed, it was well thought out and it was very worthy of winning this trip to the White House young man," Barry said smiling.

"Tho-tho..you're not mad at me th-err?" Delano asked.

"No, young man, I'm proud of you," Barry raised his hand in front of Delano to give him a high five.

"Alright, let's take a few pictures here and Carmen and Delano, we'll retreat out of this area and take a look around to the parts of the White House that are not taped off," Ursula said rolling her eyes at Barry.

Carla was waiting in the wings and stepped up to the space that was occupied by Barry and the group.

"Ah, there is Carla to take your picture Delano," Ursula said.

"Wow! That's, that's a big camera ma'am," Delano said.

Carla smiled and said: "Okay, everyone skinny up and get closer."

"Suck it in Delano!" Barry exclaimed.

Carla's camera shuttered about 10 times before she said that picture-taking time was over.

Barry shook Delano's and Carmen's hands and just before Carmen left she said to Barry: "Let's Get Crazy."

Barry gave Carmen a surprised look: "What?"

"Let's get down," Carmen said, smiled and walked out of the room.

"Did you hear her?" Barry asked Ursula.

"Hear what, sir?," Ursula asked.

"Airforce 1 is ready to go sir, we just need to get you there via the chopper," Dena said, handing him a glass of water and some Dramamine. "The Marine-One chopper will be awaiting in the East Lawn.

"Is everything alright?" Dena asked Barry.

"Where do we go?" Barry asked Dena, sidestepping her question.

Marine 1 landed on the helipad at the airport near Airforce 1. Barry exited the helicopter and he, Secretary of Defense Ashton Granger and a few of the Department of Defense team members that Ashton requested join them were on the helicopter.

The trip they were about to take was to fly up to Toronto, Canada to meet with a few US allies over the next steps they were going to take in The Middle East.

As Barry walked up the long staircase up to the entrance of Airforce 1, he couldn't get it out of his head that there was not just once, but twice now that someone uttered words to him that didn't make any sense.

He thought to himself: "What are they trying to say to me? Both statements that Jimmy Kimmel and Ms. Santiago said were Prince song titles. What the hell does that mean?"

He was greeted by a grinning flight attendant as he walked in. She introduced herself and handed him a glass of cold water.

As he sat down, one of the team members of the Department of Defense handed Barry a three-ring binder, filled with the facts, bullet points, maps, data and all things they thought Barry needed for the meeting in Toronto.

Barry loosened his bolo tie and took off his suit jacket. The same flight attendant came over and Barry handed her the jacket.

"As you can see in Tab 3, there are a lot of different data points that show that we need to take action..." Ashton said.

"Can we just take off first before we get into the specifics?" Barry asked, as he was just trying to buy time to get his head around the weirdness that was going on around him.

The pilot came on over the intercom:

"Welcome to Airforce 1 Mr. President. When we land, I'll stop by and shake your hand, until then, sit back, relax and enjoy the short 1.5 hour flight up to beautiful Toronto, Canada."

Barry was sitting in one of the luxurious sofa chairs that had an executive-like table inside it. It was the bigger of the rooms on Airforce 1. CNN, FOX News, ESPN and a few other channels were on several of the TVs inside that room.

Airforce 1 gained momentum as it chugged down the runway. The speed of the massive airplane going faster and faster until gravity was replaced with the simple gliding of the beast into the crisp fall DC air.

After 10 minutes of flying the pilot came on the intercom to say that they were at cruising altitude.

"Alright, now can we get back to business Mr. President?" Ashton asked Barry.

Barry nodded and Ashton slapped the three-ring binder down on the coffee table in front of Barry.

"Okay, as you can see in tab 3, there is a ton of data that shows we must, not 'kinda' or 'sorta', but we must get more troops into The Middle East," Ashton said.

"Or else what?" Barry said, taking a sip of his cold water.

"Or else what?? Or else we'll let those sons of bitches get away!" Ashton said.

Just as Barry was about to start talking, they felt a huge force charge through the plane.

"What the hell was that?" Barry asked Ashton.

"Just a little bit of turbulence sir, nothing to be…" Ashton was interrupted with another force of turbulence.

"Nothing to be what Mr. Ashton?" Barry rhetorically said.

Ashton was holding onto a fresh glass of scotch and the third bout of turbulence sent some of it out of the fancy china glass.

"Um, Mr. President, we're going to ask that if you're not seated…" the pilot came on the intercom as another wave of turbulence hit the plane. "…um yeah, just get buckled in, we're going to go up a bit more to find some smoother air."

They both stood up and staggered over to the next room that has more protection mechanisms inside it: no hard edges, cushion on the walls and more importantly, pilot buckles.

Barry sat down in one of the chairs and Ashton sat next to him. They both started to strap themselves into the plane when yet another huge, harder than the rest of them, waves of turbulence warped inside Airforce 1.

"Is this normal?" Barry asked Ashton.

"Uh…sure?" Ashton lied as he took a bigger gulp of his scotch.

"I read some of what you gave me Ashton, and I have to say that I don't agree that we need to do more than get more fact about …." Barry was interrupted with another gigantic wave of turbulence.

The plane started to maneuver differently than Barry had ever experienced before.

"What the hell is going on up there!" Barry exclaimed.

All of a sudden the plane started to descend a bit.

"I better go up and see what is going on," Ashton said, taking the last of his scotch and unbuckling himself.

He staggered up to the cockpit and opened the doors.

More turbulence, more maneuvering of the plane. The plane continued to descend and an alert started to sound around the entire plane.

The plane descended faster and faster, losing altitude and making Barry begin to feel very scared about what was happening.

Barry began to sing a traditional Coast Salish song to try and settle his nerves. Sweat poured down his face and he began to shake all over.

A voice came over the intercom; and that voice was not Captain Davis, whom he heard speak just before take-off. That voice was Ashton's voice:

"Sir, just to let you know that Captain Davis just had a heart attack and second Captain O'Donnell is up here and the both of us are going to get us to Toronto post haste."

What the hell? Ashton can fly planes too? Barry hadn't drank in a few years as he decided to quit over the 'Bathroom and Cell Phone' fiasco that happened in Charlotte, North Carolina when he was the President of the National Congress of American Indians.

He felt that this plane ride, perhaps his last one, warranted a nice glass of Tequila Ley, which a shot of it costs the average person $3,400 each.

Barry unbuckled himself and staggered over to the bar area outside the room he was in. He didn't care if he got it all over the place, he needed to get it inside him ASAP.

113

"Might as well take a few shots of this," Barry thought and he managed to pour himself one shot, whisked it to the back of his thoat and into his stomach.

The cold tequila went down smooth like melted butter. Almost immediately, he could feel the effects of the premium alcohol.

On his way back into the safety room, he grabbed himself some peanuts, some Dorito's, a beer and plopped them all onto the seat where Ashton was sitting.

He strapped himself in and now that the alcohol was taking effect, he was actually starting to enjoy the massive waves of turbulence that was happening.

17 minutes later, the turbulence had smoothed out. The on-board paramedic was able to control Captain Davis's vitals in the infirmary and he was now in stable condition.

Ashton decided to go back and check in on the President. As he got closer and closer to the safety room, he could hear someone or some *thing* singing in there. He opened the door and the President was clearly sloshed:

My loneliness is killing me

I must confess, I still believe….STILL BELIEVE

When I'm not with you, I lose my mind

Give me a sign…HIT ME BABY ONE MORE TIME!!

"Brittany Spears, Mr. President?" Ashton asked.

"Yeah, what's so wrong with Brittany Spears?" The President said as he had a beer in one hand and peanuts were all over

114

the place. "I mean, she's hot, she's got a voice and she never got the respect that she deserved!

"Now go get me another shot of that 'To-kill-ya' in the next room..Hit Me Baby One More Time!!" The President said as he hunched over and passed out.

"Oh, baby baby..." Ashton said shaking his head in disappointment.

All of a sudden Barry woke up in a dark room.

"Hello? Where am I?" Barry said in the quiet darkness of the room.

No one answered.

The phone rang and he noticed he was in a hotel room. He felt around for the light switch and turned on the lamp next to the bed. The phone was ringing very loudly; what he would've given for a hammer at that time to pound the hell out of it.

"HELLO?!" Barry yelled into the handset.

"Mr. President, are you okay?" It was Ursula calling in after she heard of the issues they had up in the air.

"Awe, are you calling to check in on me?" Barry asked.

"It's my job sir, the Press will be calling me any second," Ursula said.

"Yeah..yeah..I'm alright...a little hungover, but I'm alright," Barry said, yawning.

"Okay, good, listen, take care yourself, lots of water and lots of B-12s to get you through your meeting tonight okay?" Ursula instructed.

"Tonight? That meeting is tonight? I thought it was in the morning?" Barry was not happy and a bit confused.

"Yup, all of the delegates will be arriving to your hotel in about 2 hours, so wash up and get down there," Ursula said. "Did Ashton give you the de-brief?"

"Uh, yeah, he did. We went over it. We're good!" Barry said, even though it was a little white lie.

Barry rushed over to the restroom and began to take an Indian Shower, which meant: wash your face, put water on your hair and brush it out nice and smoothly; rinse with mouthwash, spray on some deodorant and spritz on some cologne.

He went to his closet and pulled out his clothes. All of his clothes were already dry cleaned and ironed.

"Ahhh..it's good to be the king," Barry said, licking his lips and rubbing his hands together.

He put on his new chonies, his undershirt and began to put on his second layer of clothes: suit pants, dress shirt and signature bolo tie.

He put his hair in a 'pony' and sat down to catch his breath. He looked up at the clock: "Yup, in record time!" referring to his time it took to get ready.

Just as he was looking around the medicine cabinet for some aspirin or something to cure the throbbing headache he created, he heard a knock at the door.

Barry opened the hotel room door.

"Hi, my name is Nancy and I am the hotel general manager. I just want to extend a heartfelt welcome to you and your team and thank you for choosing our hotel to have your meeting," she said extending her hand for a handshake.

Barry looked at one of the secret servicemen who was standing just to Nancy's left. The agent nodded and Barry extended his hand out and shook it.

"Thanks for having us; but, can I trouble you for something?" Barry asked.

"Here's two aspirin, two B-12s and a caffeine pill," Nancy said handing Barry the assortment of pills. "An Ursula called us a few minutes ago and that is the other reason I came up here."

"You-are-a-Lifesaver!!" Barry said slowly.

He wished her a good day and retreated back into the hotel room. He poured himself a glass of fresh water, placed all five pills in his mouth and gulped them all down.

He was so thirsty that he poured himself another cup of water and gulped that down too.

Barry looked at himself in the mirror and took three deep breaths. He straightened out his bolo tie and said a small prayer and walked out the door towards the make-shift 'war room' that his team created to get ready for the meeting.

Chapter 12: On the Road Again

Barry's cell phone rings and on the third ring, Barry hits the send button.

"Hello?" Barry says.

"Mr. President, where are you?" Dena asks.

"I'm at the train station, where are you?" he asks.

"I'm at my desk, sir, but why are you at the train station?" she replies.

"..be-cause I'm taking the train back to DC," he says.

"A train sir?" she asks.

"Yes, you know, the ones that go 'choo choo?' he says smiling.

"But sir, Airforce 1 is fueled up and ready for your return trip back to the White House," she advises.

"After last night's fiasco, I don't think I'm ever going to fly again," Barry says and plops a piece of gum into his mouth.

"I heard that you had a rough flight," she empathized with him.

"Rough? You call that shit show, rough?" Barry rhetorically asks. "That flight caused me to drink again and I don't do that normally."

"I heard about that too," she confessed.

"Well, that's it for this guy, no more flights. Heck, the train ain't bad, I can still do my work from the caboose, they serve a heck of a meal and better yet, no risk of dying!" Barry exclaimed.

Barry hung up the phone as he heard the announcement that his train going west from the northeast was ready to board. Of course the paparazzi was all lined up just outside of the caboose that Barry was about to get into.

He was blinded by the flashbulbs and the questions that they were all asking was a bit deafening.

The secret service agents all got in before him and secured the space he would be occupying in the next day. It would a day to go from Toronto, Canada to Washington, DC, after the Amtrak they were taking was going to be stopping in a few spots prior to getting to DC.

Barry's team set up a make-shift war room in one of the two cabooses they commandeered to ensure Barry could still work from the train.

Barry sat down on the train's bench chairs and made himself comfortable. Amtrak ensured that the President had a few dedicated servers to accommodate him throughout the time he was on the train.

"Would you like something to eat, sir?" said the Amtrak server.

He thought about it for a second... "Um, no, that will be okay, I don't need anything yet," he said.

Just as he was getting comfortable, a knock on his caboose door sounded. He opened up the door and it was a tall slender young man on the other side.

"Hello?" Barry said.

"Hi sir, my name is Jerry, Jerry Imhoff and I am going to be assisting you during this trip back to DC," he said.

"Jerry Imhoff..how do I know that name?" Barry asked and sat down.

"I work for New York Senator Bernie Sherman but we got a phone call early this morning from DC asking if we could 'donate' a person to come and assist you and to ensure you made it back to DC ok," Jerry said.

"Assist me? More like babysit me..." Barry said, turning on the TV in his box car.

"Well, I'll be in the next box car over if you need anything, just push this button; it's an intercom that goes right into the area that I'll be in on the train," Jerry said, standing back up and making his way out of Barry's space.

A few minutes later, Jerry was again knocking on Barry's door.

"Sir, you have a phone call, it's the Secretary of State Heather Youngman, would you like to take it?" Jerry asked.

"Please transfer it to my desktop phone right there," Barry said, pointing at the big, black phone with what seemed like a million buttons on it.

The phone rang and rang and Barry had no idea how to answer it. Jerry came running back into Barry's box car and pushed the big red button that had the word 'ON' written on top of it.

"This is Barry," he said. Jerry excused himself as Barry sat down. "What's going on?"

"Mr. President, we're on a secure line, so it's okay to be open and honest about what it is that I am calling you about," Youngman said.

"Okay, what it all about?" Barry asked.

"We need to choose and confirm the next Vice President of the United States," she said. "The meeting you had earlier today in Toronto and more importantly, the flight you had

120

last night are prime examples that we need to fast track the process of naming a new Vice President," she said.

"Okay, what's the process?" he reluctantly asked.

"We will get the full Cabinet ready for you to meet with them as soon as possible. Your train is set to arrive in DC at 0800 hours tomorrow morning and a caravan will take you directly to the White House. We'll give you time to shower and shave and eat some breakfast; so we'll set the meeting up for 11-00 hours, okay?" she asked.

He agreed and hung up the phone. A few hours of channel surfing and internet searching made him feel sleepy. He stretched and yawned and before he knew it, he was out like a light.

A few minutes later, the train came to a complete stop. He stood up and wandered outside of his box car and into the hallway of the train.

"Hello? Is anyone out here?" Barry asked.

No answer.

"Hello?!! Jerry? Anyone?"

Still no answer.

He began to look into every box car and each of the rooms were completely empty. He got scared and his heart began to pound. He began to sweat as he continued to be alone on the train.

Barry got up to the front of the train, where the conductor was and there was a small man standing there waiting for him.

"Hello Mr. President, your party is waiting for you outside," said the train conductor.

Barry looked very confused and asked the conductor, "What party?"

The conductor opened up the train's front door and exposed the thousands of people that were outside gathered. He took a few steps down from the train and onto the ground.

While looking around, the entire makeup of the audience was a diversity of Native Americans; each wearing their regalia and either had a hand drum, rattle or large drum.

He could see the representation of tribes from all over the globe: Navajo, Cree, Coast Salish, Hawaiian, South American, Pequot.

They were all staring at him with no signs of any expression except their 'neutral' faces.

A thin layer of fog had crept into the area and he could smell a little bit of gun powder in the air.

"Hello?" Barry said.

No one answered him, they all just continued to stare.

"My name is Barry," he said. "The President of the United States..."

Barry began to speak in Lah-shoot-seed (language mostly spoken by members of the Tulalip Tribes).

In unison, the entire audience began to sing a song, starting out in a baritone voice and using their soprano-like voices in between the baritones. Using their traditional 'instruments,' they began to accompany the beautiful singing.

Barry walked into the crowd, watching in awe of the thousands upon thousands of people that were there, all singing in one voice. He passed by elders, babies, women, young men, children, Rez dogs and even more astonishing, tall, big ape looking men that he thought looked like sasquatch.

The song became louder and louder with each verse. All of a sudden, the song went from a traditional one to a more contemporary one.

The traditional native chorus changed to a contemporary song that he really knew: "When Doves Cry,"….

….'*this is what it sounds like when dove's cry,…*' they sang in unison.

Barry woke up from his dream in a pool of sweat.

"Excuse me sir, would you like some dinner?" asked the Amtrak server.

"Huh? What?" Barry said, wiping off the sweat from his face. "Uh, sure, yes, let me wash up; where's the restroom?"

The Amtrak team member ushered Barry out of his box car and into the hallway. Barry could see all the many people on the train and began to smile and chuckle a bit to know that he had himself a dream.

Inside the restroom, he loosened up his bolo tie and rolled up his long white sleeves. He turned on the faucet and began to wash his hands and his face.

He looked at himself in the mirror and said under his breath:

"When Dove's Cry?!"

Barry thought to himself: 'why in the hell does he have these snippets of Prince songs either said to him in real life or in dreams?'

He dried himself off and made his way back to his area where waiting for him near his chair was a plate with a hot cover on it. He opened up the hot cover and exposed turkey, mashed potatoes and gravy with green beans.

Barry sat down and began to eat into the beautifully presented plate of food.

12 hours later, Barry arrived in Washington D.C. Again, a paparazzi of photographers was there to take every image of him getting off the train. Barry shook hands with a few people who were cleared to be in that area by security who cordoned off the area.

A large black Escalade was awaiting the arrival of the President and he got into it which ushered him directly to the White House.

He said hello to the White House team, who were all anxiously awaiting his arrival.

Barry went up to his room and put everything away. He changed his clothes and went into the Executive boardroom where the entire cabinet was standing awaiting his arrival.

"You may all have a seat," Barry said as he himself grabbed the last remaining chair located in the middle of the table. "I understand from talking to Secretary of State Youngman that we must name a Vice President?"

"Yes, Mr. President, we think it's been long enough without one and we must ensure that our democracy may go forward in the event that..." Barry interrupted Youngman.

"That what? That I die?" Barry said looking down at the table smiling.

"Well.., well,..yes sir, we just think that..." Youngman said.

"I agree," Barry interrupted her again. "I think it's time."

"So, who do you nominate Mr. President?" asked the Secretary of Treasury Dorothy Pinnicle.

"Well, Ms. Pinnicle, I originally was going to go for Harry Ostreiler, but he decided that moving from Washington State to Washington DC was not in his or his wife's best interest. Therefore, I nominate Yvonne Underwood," Barry said. He lifted both hands as he began to speak. "She has done an amazing job in Texas, raising minimum wages for all workers and especially equaling wages for women to match all men there. She is a helluva person and someone I think we'll all have a great time getting to know better and working with."

Secretary of Treasury Pinnicle, Attorney General Reatha Randolph, Secretary of Interior Irene Polomon, Secretary of Agriculture Danielle Osterman and Secretary of Commerce Phillip Ryder all agreed with Barry and all had sensational things to say about Underwood.

There were several other candidates that the group talked about but in the end, it was Barry's choice and in the end his choice of the Governor of Texas, Yvonne Underwood would be the person that would be named the 46th Vice President of the United States.

Barry and the cabinet would take the recommendation to the House and the Senate to get ratified and a month after this historic meeting, Yvonne Underwood was sworn in as the Vice President of the United States.

"It's a pleasure and an honor to work with you Mr. President," Underwood said as she shook Barry's hand. Barry had called for their first official meeting to discuss next steps in every area and to get her caught up on all issues regarding the United States.

They both walked into the war room as some of the members of the President's Cabinet were there: Secretary of Labor Thomas Monty, Secretary of Health and Human Services Kell Borenstein, Secretary of Housing Fred Valentine and Secretary of Commerce Phillip Ryder were at the table along with technical team members of the Oval Office were all there to help Underwood get caught up.

After shaking all of their hands, Underwood herself took a seat to hear the presentation. She had with her a nice leather bound notepad that she traditionally used while serving as the Governor of Texas.

Underwood was always seen holding a notepad in her hand and was notorious for writing in details of new information that she would get from other elected officials or her constituents, many of whom would stop her while she was out and about in various cities like Austin.

Standing at the front of the room was newly hired Chief of Staff Harmony Christensen. Harmony, was a tribal member from Navajo whom the President met at a fundraiser. Many of those who were in attendance of that fundraiser knew that the President was looking for someone who knew policy, that had a great team-like presence and could communicate well.

Harmony had worked in a few of the Cabinet offices prior to being named the President's Chief of Staff. She was known for her work ethic, attention to detail and she spoke Navajo fluently.

"Good morning Mrs. Vice President," Harmony said. "It's a pleasure and honor to be working alongside of you."

Underwood looked up from her notepad and flashed a big smile and a nod at Harmony.

"We've designed this presentation to give you as much detail about each of the topics without inundating you with too much information," Harmony said, her dark brown skin and dark long black hair covering part of the gray suit she was wearing. She wore abalone shell earrings and a traditional turquoise necklace.

Harmony and the rest of them went through a 4-hour presentation, going through key topics of the economy, education, healthcare, international affairs and more.

Barry ensured that Underwood's questions were being answered to the best of his ability and to ensure that all details were given to her as much as they could possibly be.

"Any more questions Ms. Underwood?" Harmony asked.

"Wow, it looks like you all have done a masterful job here in the White House," Underwood said closing up her notepad, which was now almost completely full of notes.

Underwood stood up and the rest of the room also stood up. Barry walked over to where she was standing.

"Let's arrange dinner tonight here in my dining room, please bring along your husband,…Harry is his name right?" Barry asked.

"Yes, Harry is his name," Underwood said. "He's back at the house awaiting my arrival. He is just as amazed at all of this as I am. I mean we were just married a few weeks ago and now this?"

"Okay, we'll meet at 7 p.m. tonight, okay?" Barry said.

"7 it is, Mr. President," Underwood said and put out her hand to shake his hand.

He reached over and gave her a hug instead. "Sorry, I'm a hugger."

Chapter 13: One Down, Three Left

It has now been one year since Barry was thrusted into the White House. As he was getting ready to attend a one-year anniversary party that he wanted to put together, he began to think how he got into politics.

It was 1982 and he was a student at Western Washington University, having received a full scholarship from Boeing and The Warren Buffet Foundation.

Barry majored in Political Science with a minor in Communications. He was a B+ average student and he was his own biggest critic.

He'd drive home from Bellingham, WA to the Tulalip reservation a few times a month. The short 45-minute drive was just long enough to feel like he wasn't sucking on his mom's teat but short enough to make it home for dinner with his parents if needed.

It was one night while sitting at the dinner table with his parents that he got the bug to run for political office.

"I'm so tired of the way the administration treats us Natives at Western," Barry said, taking a big bite of goulash (a mixture of green beans, rice, hamburger and tomato rice) and using a piece of frybread to help scoop it up on the fork and into his mouth.

"Then do something about it," his dad uttered, which to this day Barry would never forget.

His dad, Larry Whiteman was an employee at a local saw mill and had been there for over 20 years. Larry had gained the respect of the other guys in the union after going head to head with the CEO of the saw mill over wages.

When Larry uttered the words: 'then-do-something', he stared right into his son's eyes which stung Barry like a bee deep into his soul.

Barry put the fork and bread down and nodded his head. He gulped down the mouthful of goulash and stood up.

"Yes, yes, that's what I'll do, I'll run for student president!" Barry said.

"You'll never make it!" said Don, Barry's younger brother and pain in Barry's side.

"Shut up Don, go back to the tree house with your other pee-ons," Barry said, throwing the remains of his frybread at him.

Don ducked the frybread tossing and retaliated with his own throw of frybread that struck Barry in the forehead.

"Guys!" their father said with his deep baritone voice which got the attention of both boys. They both settled down and began to eat again.

"You can do whatever you put your mind to," Barry's mom Trina said. Trina Whiteman was the youngest of five sisters in her family. She was about 10 years younger than Larry and was a stay-at-home mother to the two boys.

Trina was always the voice of reason when Barry needed it. As Barry was putting on his tie to go to the one-year anniversary party at the White House, he thought how much his mom would've loved to attend this party.

During Barry's freshman year at Western, he got a bit homesick. Even though he was a short drive away from home, it had been the first time he lived away from the reservation.

Back then, he didn't own a car, so he would have to arrange trips back to Tulalip either by train, bus or if a classmate who lived in Seattle would drive him to the freeway exit that lead to the Tulalip reservation.

He remembers almost dropping out of school and even made up his mind that he was going to drop out. When Barry made up his mind, 99% of the time, he normally followed through on it.

"You-are-not-going-to-drop-out!" Trina said over the phone one winter night to Barry.

"But mom, I'm missing out on so much down there," Barry said wiping a tear from his eye.

"You are going to finish what you start, do I make myself clear?" Trina asked.

Barry was silent.

Trina could've went on a tirade and bombarded him with a ton of stories about how so-and-so did this and so-and-so did that and each one ending with how they never gave up. Instead, Trina had a way of mentoring her sons so that it sounded like a great idea.

"Listen son," Trina slowed down the speed of her next words. "You are one of the brightest persons I know. You have a heart of gold. Both your heart and your mind need more time to develop and by being there at Western, you are showing yourself that you are not a quitter, that you will give it all up and sacrifice your current life for one that is better."

Barry started to tear up even more.

"But what about you guys, I mean I feel like I'm missing out on life with you, dad and that little booger," Barry said referring to his younger brother.

"We'll be here, even that little booger will be here," Trina paused. "We'll always be here."

Barry went to the White House mirror and began to fix his bolo tie. A tear welted up in his eye and he quickly wiped it away.

The words, 'we'll always be here,' rung into Barry's mind. He felt a slight anger in his body after hearing those words again.

It was a few months after Barry had hung up the phone that night that the good Lord took Larry, Trina and his brother Don in a fatal car accident in Tulalip.

The three of them had just left the Marysville Pilchuck High School where Liz, Barry's cousin, had just gave an amazing presentation during the annual debate competition.

They were heading home and it had been snowing very heavily in the greater Everett, WA area. Their car, which normally had good traction was hit head-on by an oncoming semi-truck which veered out of control due to the ice that had covered the oily roads.

Barry had been in a night class at Western, when one of the administrators, whom he was going to take to task if elected student body president, broke the news to him that his family were all laid up in the Everett Hospital.

All three of them died the next day.

A knock at the door of his room in the White House sounded. He fixed his bolo tie, wiped the remains of the tears in his eye and opened the door.

"Your family has arrived, sir," said newly-hired Rudolph, who was Barry's Executive Host inside the White House. He was named an Executive Host, rather than butler or servant for PR reasons.

"Okay, thanks Rudy, I will gather the rest of my belongings here and head down to the ballroom. Please tell them that I'll be down there shortly?" Barry asked.

"Very well, sir," Rudolph said and closed Barry's door.

Barry gave himself one more look in the mirror, combed out a little bit of a hair tangle of his long black hair which now had a bit of silver to it and headed down to the ballroom where over 1,000 people were expected to attend the celebration.

The tall ballroom doors opened and Barry entered the room. The entire guest list which consisted of Barry's team, the Cabinet and their team members, the White House team of employees, A-list celebrities and of course other elected officials were all in attendance and stood up out of respect of the head-native-in-charge (the HNIC).

The Tulalip national anthem began to ring out through the ballroom, as Barry invited the Fryberg and Wilbur families of Tulalip and Swinomish tribes to the White House for that very purpose.

Barry shook hands with almost every person that was in his path from the ballroom entrance to the head table, located just below the tall stage which was on the opposite side of the ballroom entrance.

A bright white light from a few spotlights that were in the corners of the room illuminated the President. Barry raised both hands out from his body and into the air as a symbolic gesture of his gratitude to all of them for their hard work and dedication during these past 365 days.

He finally got up to the stage and went up to the microphone. He waited until the final segments of the traditional honor song were sung and began to speak to the capacity crowd.

"Wow...wow...thank you....thank you so much for this great reception," Barry said. "How about a round of applause for my family up here who sang our incredible Tulalip national anthem?"

The entire crowd eagerly applauded and gave their appreciation.

"Tonight, we're going to party," Barry said, holding a glass of apple cider, which looked like champagne from a distance. He decided to abstain from alcohol during this event so that he could eliminate the possibilities of saying something or doing something that the media could get their hands on.

"Tonight, this is a celebration and as my late father used to say: 'son, if you have the means, if you have the desire, then let loose and take it higher' and tonight ladies and gentlemen, we're going to take it higher!"

The entire crowd erupted into applause.

"May God rest the souls of my late-parents and my little brother Don, whom I know all three of them are here with us in spirit," Barry said and again a little tear formed in his eye.

The crowd lightly applauded and the singers with their hand drum in hand banged lightly on their drums in honor of the three deceased family members.

"I'm eternally grateful for my family that is here with us, please show your appreciation for my Uncle Jack, Auntie G, cousins Charlie, Liz and Tammie!" Barry said, using his lips to point at the head table where Barry would eventually sit.

His auntie mom Zeta couldn't make the trip, as she wasn't feeling too well and didn't feel like she should travel.

All five of them raised their hands out and waved at the crowd, their image flashing on the 20' x 20' screens located around the ballroom.

"I don't know what I'd do without my family," Barry said into the microphone. "For the past 365 days since I was sworn in, you all have become my family.

"Before I go any further, I want to extend my gratitude to Martha and a few of the-late John Dungberry's family who are also in attendance tonight," Barry said again, using his lips to point at the table next to the head table.

"Family is important, it is the backbone to who I am and what I stand for," Barry said. "Our values are how we make decisions every day, it is through the lenses of values that tonight I extend my most heartfelt thank you to each of you for the fine work you do.

"Tonight, we're going to party, we're going to take it higher as dad would've said. We've got one down and three to go! Thank you! Thank you! Let's have a good time everyone!" Barry exclaimed to another round of applause.

As Barry was beginning to exit off the stage, the chants from the audience was: '7 more years! 7 more years! 7 more years!'

Just before Barry was going to go down the stack of stairs that were on the side of the stage, he was met by the night's emcee, comedian Kevin Hart.

The 5'6" Hart shook Barry's hand and Barry was genuinely surprised that he was on stage with him.

"I'm a big fan Mr. Hart," Barry said.

"I'm a big fan of yours Mr. President," Hart said smiling big.

Barry glided down the staircase and made his way to the head table, giving Martha and her family a hug or handshake.

"Wow, wow, another round of applause to the HNIC!" Hart said into the microphone.

"Yeah, I said it, the H-N-I-C...the head NATIVE in charge! Who'da thunk it? Who would've thought that this country would have a Native American in charge of the free world?

"Boy, my grand pappy would be rolling around in his grave right now. I mean, he was one of the racist mother fuckers in America. He was so racist that he hated anyone that wasn't as dark as him. He hated other African Americans, ones that were light skinned.

"He'd say, 'if you ain't got the black *ON* you, then how can I trust that black *INSIDE-A-YOU*," Hart said with a slight of hick sound in his voice, as the crowd began to laugh.

"Now, having a Red President ain't so bad? I mean, you never know when President Whiteman is mad? Has anyone ever seen our President mad? His skin won't allow us to see when he's mad or when he's embarrassed.

"I mean, when all the other presidents were mad, we'd see it. Remember, when Clinton was running for his second term and his opponent brought up Monica Lewinski? Boy, his face would turn strawberry.

"Remember when Bush number two was running for his second term and his opponent brought up Osama?

"Both of those presidents would get so strawberry in the face, we all were lookin' around for some whip cream to put on their faces," Hart said smiling and looking out into the audience as if he was really searching for some whip cream.

"Oh...but no, not when you have a Red President. Oh no...instead we get this stoic look on his face," Hart says turning into a statue and a neutral stone-face expression on his face.

"Me President. Me the Ruler of the World. Me will throw your white pasty ass in jail if you don't get out of my way," the capacity crowd busted into laughter.

Kevin Hart emceed the rest of the night and just as Barry asked in his welcome speech, the entire audience did have a blast, listening to Hart talk, live music and dancing, the best chefs making the greatest tasting food and each person receiving a small swag bag filled with luxury watches and cell phone accessories.

At the end of the night, Barry's family who drove out to DC from Washington State met him in Barry's living room area. Each were sitting on a leather sofa awaiting Barry's arrival.

"That was one helluva party son," Auntie Georgianna said taking off her low-heel shoes as Barry walked into the room.

"Yeah Auntie G? Did you all get enough to eat?" Barry asked.

"If you feed me one more bite, I swear I'm gonna explode!" exclaimed Uncle Jack.

Barry sat down and relaxed next to his family. "How was the trip out here?"

"Good, good,..only took us three days this time," said cousin Liz. "We followed directions didn't we Tammy?"

Tammy nodded.

"Son, I just want to tell you that we're all so very proud of you," Uncle Jack said. "Your dad, my brother, would've been so proud of you...you have no idea."

A tear welted up in Barry's eye again. "Crap, I've been crying all frickin' night thinking of them. I guess I haven't released the build-up in my heart?"

"Gotsta let them go son," Aunt G said, whipping her sweaty stockings in the air creating a smell that was a cross between Frito Lay's chips and day-old eggs.

Wiping away the tear and moving his head away from the waft, Barry shook his head in agreement.

"They in a better place now, and one day we'll all meet them in the pearly gates!" Aunt G said.

Barry stood up and said: "Ok guys, have a restful night, I'll see you all in the morning for breakfast!"

He gave them each a hug and made his way out of the room and into his bedroom.

Chapter 14: Time to Go on Offense

The entire Presidential cabinet was gathered in the Executive Boardroom awaiting the President's arrival. Some of the cabinet members were in the corners of the boardroom, having their own side bar meetings.

Barry walked into the Boardroom and the entire team stood up in response to his arrival.

"Please, please, be seated," Barry said and took a seat at his normal chair, located in the middle of the table.

Barry was dressed in a button up shirt, jeans and no bolo tie. The meeting was supposed to be a retreat of some sort, a way for his entire team to use their creative minds to help bring more resources and carve out some time for the President to do what he could do here at home.

"Good morning everyone," Barry addressed the team. "This morning and for the next two days, I want us to carve out some time to figure out how we can meet the needs of the American people here at home.
"I know we've been spending some time away from the US, dealing with many international issues that are much needed, but here at home, we have so much to do.

"We've heard the rhetoric for so many years about the big issues: education, health care, unemployment, and so forth. I, along with the late John Dungberry, ran a campaign for President that stated that status quo was not going to be a part of the work that we, or now, I would do for the American public.

"So, I want us to think outside-the-box, in fact, toss the box, throw it out and let's start with a clean sheet of paper. How can we really meet the needs of the people; how can we really cut through the bureaucratic bull crap that has plagued our great country for far too long?

"No idea is bad; no idea is off-limits. We will need every idea, every comment and every person in this room to share his or her idea; does everyone understand what I'm saying?" Barry asked.

The entire cabinet peered back at Barry as if they had seen a ghost.

"Hello?" Barry asked one more time.

Finally, the entire room erupted in chatter, many of them shouting out their idea and the decibel level in the room reached as high as a Seahawks home game.

Barry stood up: "Whoa...! Okay, okay, everyone, great energy! Love the energy! Now we need some order here because I want us to all have the opportunity to share what is in our hearts and in our minds.

"Dena?..." Barry looked around to find his assistant. Dena walked in and she had with her a pile of papers that she was about to distribute.

"Dena will be giving you all a packet of information; most of the packet, however, does contain questions that I want to ask and if you would be so kind, we'll be taking a lot of time to allow you the opportunity to write in an answer to each question.

"Then, when you're called upon, you'll have up to 2 minutes to state your creative idea; this is an ooooold Indian tactic that we've been using for quite sometime in Indian Country.

"We learned our lesson letting some of the tribal politicians in the room have far too long to share their ideas; it got to the point where we would only hear from half of the room, rather than the entire floor.

"So, we developed this as a way for us to hear from every single person, their idea to the solutions that we need to have to make our communities better," Barry said and sat back down.

Barry made sure every person had a packet of information and for the next 3.5 hours, before lunch, he followed along the information in the packet and asked each of them to fill in the blanks.

Stretching and standing up, Barry said: "Okay, gang, good job. How's everyone's brain doing right now?"

Many of the cabinet members started to yawn and stretch their backs and a few of them stood up along with Barry.

"Let's take a 2-hour lunch and I'll see you all back here at 1 PM?" Barry rhetorically asked and began to walk out of the Boardroom.

Outside of the Boardroom in the pre-function area, Barry had the White House chef prepare a gourmet buffet meal for the team. He asked Ashton Granger, the Secretary of Defense to say a pre-meal prayer, which he obliged.

One-by-one, they all grabbed a hot plate and began to receive a scoop of food from each of the banquet dishes.

Barry watched as each of them grabbed their lunch and he retreated back into the Boardroom where he sat down and began to mull over the next steps that the team would make at the 1 PM hour.

A team member was at the Boardroom door and knocked on the door frame because the Boardroom doors were open.

"Are you going to eat Mr. President?" asked Carla, the White House photographer.

"Oh, hi Carla, I forgot you were even here," Barry said, telling somewhat-of-a-lie. He could hear her shooting pictures throughout the first half of the day's retreat, plus, he always did find her attractive and put on a little bit of a show every time she was around.

"Yup, I'm here, I'm always peering around the corner, capturing as many moments of your tenure as I can," she said somewhat blushing.

She sat down next to him: "I just want to tell you that I think you're doing a fantastic job, Mr. President."

"Barry, please call me Barry," he said looking down with his charismatic smile.

"Well, Barry, I just want to tell you that I think the work you've done so far, you know, only a year into your term, has been an honor and a privilege to be around," she said.

"Thank you Carla, I really do appreciate the compliment. It really is a team effort; I inherited a great cabinet, a fantastic White House group of people and the world's best photographer," he complimented her again.

"I was wondering, ...Mr....I mean, Barry, if you would want to...well,.."Carla began to ask him a question when another voice interrupted her.

"Mr. President?" It was Ursula, who had come to the Boardroom to ask Barry a question. "Ooops, sorry, should I come back?"

Her interruption cut the tension in half and Barry stood up a bit awkwardly, quickly got his composure and invited Ursula in.

"No, no, this is a good time to come in, what may I do you for?" Barry asked Ursula.

She came in and stood by Carla's chair: "The Today's Show is asking for you to do an interview via satellite for tomorrow morning's show, how shall we proceed."

Barry looked at Ursula, but his attention quickly went to Carla's face as he began to answer Ursula's question.

"The Today's Show huh?" Barry said smiling. "I always liked that show, I like how it seems that the women of that show seem to get older and Matt seems to stay the same age, how does he do that?"

Carla looked down smiling from ear-to-ear. She always loved the way he thought and how he spoke, in private as well as when he was interviewed by the press.

It was clear to Ursula that throughout their back-and-forth question, then answer during this small amount of time that something was going on underneath between the President and Carla.

She could tell that Carla was indeed a distraction to the President and that his demeanor was more candid, more playful and more relaxed when she was around.

Ursula left the Boardroom with her questions answered and she also got the hint that she wasn't the only one that was interested in having a less plutonic relationship with the President.

Later in the day, she found it a bit odd that in the beginning, she didn't think Barry was that attractive; his long black hair, his round brown eyes, his semi-dark skin, with wrinkles around his temple area; the way he walked, the way he talked, was all so different.

She didn't ever think he wasn't attractive, but he was different; he came from the Pacific Northwest, had a passive aggressive demeanor about him, which drove Ursula crazy because on the east coast, where she is from, they just come out and say what is on their minds.

Maybe it was Barry's power that he now possessed as the leader of the free world. Maybe it was his tribal lineage that after a year of working alongside of him, she began to find romantic.

Whatever it all was, it took having Carla, who herself was a very attractive woman, to make Ursula believe that she was falling in love with the President.

It was now 1 PM and the entire team was already settled into their seats awaiting Barry's arrival. Right at 1 PM on the dot, Barry walked in and the entire team stood up again.

Barry closed the door behind him and he and the entire team sat down. He rolled up his sleeves and began to talk: "Okay gang, let's get to business. We spent 3.5 hours writing down the answers to the questions that I posed."

He asked Jerry Imhoff, the former assistant to Senator Bernie Sherman, whom he met on the Amtrak train to become his Executive Assistant, to moderate the next few hours of the work plan that they would develop.

"Good afternoon ladies and gentleman, my name is Jerry, you can call me by my given name or as President Whiteman calls me, you have my permission to call me J-dog, just don't call me late for dinner," he said smiling waiting for someone to at least give a small chuckle. "Okay, tough audience; I want to commend each of you for taking the last 3 or so hours to come with ideas that will make America better, so without further ado, let's get to work."

For the next four hours, each of the cabinet and White House team members, including the housekeeping team, were asked to give their answers to questions like this:

If you were President, what would you change first?

If you had limitless amounts of money, how would you use it to make America better?

What injustices do you see that needs to change immediately?

It was now 5:30 p.m. and they pushed through that part of the session with no breaks, as Barry put it when asked during the session if they could have a break: "We didn't take breaks when I was Chairman of the Tulalip Tribes because we knew that we had work to get done; plus if we did, it would take too long to get back into session, so no, let's push through."

When the President excused them, after taking what many in the room thought was a long time to thank them, many of them ran out of the room to go use the restroom or to go light up a cigarette.

Barry excused them until the next morning, where they would pick up where they left off. During dinner, Barry met with his small inner circle of team members that he would rely on and trust with everything he would do next.

The small group consisted of: Harmony Christensen (Chief of Staff), Jerry Imhoff, Vice-President Yvonne Underwood and Ursula.

"So, what did you think of today's session Barry?" Yvonne asked him.

Hesitating before speaking, Barry finally said: "I'm pissed off."

A shocked look ran across the faces of the small group.

"Really?" Yvonne asked him.

Barry's face began to get a little red: "Yeah, Yvonne. I'm pissed off that the answers that each of them gave are the same frickin' answers that I've heard in every meeting, every gathering; it's the same rhetoric that John and the rest of the Presidential candidates spoke about over a year ago.

"We've trained our teams over the years to believe in the same garbage, that have been spoken from Nixon to Obama!"

Barry stood up and walked over to the end of the table where there was a pitcher of water and a few empty unused glassware and began to pour himself a glass of ice water.

He took a gulp and said: "When are we going to really make change for America?"

"Give us some examples Barry, tell us what you really mean," Yvonne asked.

He walked over to the Boardroom wall next to the front door where Jerry had been writing on the 'writeable walls' with a dry-erase pen.

"Look at it here, when asked what would they do if they were the President of the United States, the best answer they could come up with was that they would increase taxes for the rich and cut taxes for the poor.

"Or look at this one, they would remove carbon emissions to protect the environment.

"What the hell!! This group of people have been brainwashed into the same rhetoric, the same way of thinking that has been going on for over one hundred years!"

The room went completely quiet, for the first time since Barry took office, he lost his composure.

No one wanted to ask him anything, say anything and the tension in the room was deafening.

He sat back down: "I'm sorry, I didn't mean to lose my temper. I am just so-sick-and-tired of hearing the same old, same old..these thoughts that they have were not original, they were duplicate messages that they have heard every candidate from the county to the White House say over and over again."

"So, what do we do Mr. President? How do we get them un-brainwashed?" Yvonne asked him.

Slouching in his chair, his eyes got wide and he stood back up: "I know exactly what we'll do,...."

The entire room was waiting on the next moments that would probably occupy their time for the next 'x' amount of weeks or months.

"We'll do exactly what we did when I was the President of the National Congress of American Indians," he said. "We'll take our team on the road, and *show* them what is happening in America."

"Show them sir?" Yvonne was a bit confused.

"Yes, Yvonne, we'll show them what needs to get done in America. One of my mentors told me, the best way to learn is to go there, feel it, or as he called it...*look, listen and learn,*" Barry said going up to a map of America that was posted on the Boardroom wall.

He pointed to every state and said that he and the team 'would go by bus and we'll visit every state and we'll talk to residents and ask them the same questions that we were asked.'

Barry heard every rebuttal to this idea, every excuse, every reason why they shouldn't do this. Most Presidents or CEOs, would be upset that his inner circle would try and talk the idea down, but not Barry; he enjoyed hearing why they shouldn't do an idea.

Even after the 35-minute rant from his team as to why his idea was 'ludicrous', 'irresponsible,' 'not safe,' he decided to make his decision based on his gut instinct.

"Thank you, everyone for trying to talk me off the ledge on this idea, however, an elder of mine once said that if it feels uncomfortable, then that is the best answer to go with," he said smiling. "Jerry, make the arrangements, we'll go by bus to every state and even if we spend just an hour with residents, we'll ask them the same or similar questions that we were asked and we'll get our answers in 50 days."

"Got it, sir," Jerry said and bolted out of the Boardroom.

"Ursula, get the talking points ready and set up a briefing on the south lawn for tomorrow morning, we're going on the offensive!"

Barry left the Boardroom and those who were still left in the room all slouched in their chairs, exhausted from the meeting; some were confused, some were speechless and a few were visibly upset.

They weren't mad or confused because they didn't feel that they were not heard, they were feeling this way because they were going into the unknown.

What former President had ever done this? They were used to candidates running for President going into regions and speaking to hundreds of thousands of Americans to capture their votes but no President in history, had ever went state-by-state and asked the Americans for their input like Barry was directing them to do.

"Good evening, and welcome to the Wolfe Blitzer Show, my name is Janice Thompson, filling in for Wolfe. With me tonight are my good friends, David Satler and James Blufield and gentleman, thank you for coming on with me.

"Can you believe what we heard in this morning's White House briefing by President Whiteman? He told us that he and his cabinet are taking the show on the road in what he calls the "50 days of Enlightenment."

"I think the President has lost it," said Blufield, smiling as he talked. "He must be smoking the hippie lettuce that is legal in his home State of Washington."

"I agree Janice," Satler said. "Does he understand the implications, I mean what if the South Koreans or ISIS get their hands on when and where the President will be? He'll be a sitting duck!"

"Well, if the President does get hurt or worse off killed during this campaign, Vice President Underwood would be sworn in as our next President," Thompson said.

"And who is our Vice President?" Satler asked. "I mean, she was sworn in behind closed doors, none of us were asked if she would make a good Vice President, I mean like it was said, the President has lost it if he thinks that this 50 Days of dog and pony show is going to work with the voting public."

"Let's talk about that for a minute, guys, the latest Gallup Poll is out and it shows that President Whiteman's satisfaction numbers are up. As you can see in this chart, his satisfaction percentage was in the 40th percentile a few months ago and now is over 50 percent at 51, so I pose this question to the both of you," Thompson said. "Is this '50 days campaign' a publicity stunt or do you think he authentically wants to know what the public thinks they should be working on?"

"I think it's both," Blufield said. "I think he does see that by going state-to-state, that he and his team could gain the public's trust. Yet, in talking to people of his inner circle, they say he believes that he is authentic; regardless of what we think of him."

"I disagree, Janice," Satler said. "I think it's all a publicity stunt, I mean, no President has ever done this, why should we believe that he is authentically wanting to do the right thing here?"

"Well, time will tell and we'll see what happens as the President and his entire team will fly over to Hawaii and begin the 50 days in the Aloha state," Thompson said.

Chapter 15: Aloooooha!

Secretary of State Youngman, Secretary of Homeland Security Ian Ettman, Chief of Staff Christensen and National Security Advisor Rasmussen quickly created and executed the road map that Barry and the entire Cabinet would follow as the best and safest route for all of them.

Barry wanted to start in Hawaii, as it was now early-November and most of the country was in a lot of snow or cold weather. Inclement weather was one of the many reasons that his inner circle said why they shouldn't do this campaign.

Hawaii in November, if you've never been there during that month is quite delightful. The temperatures hover in the mid-70's and most locals wear long-sleeve shirts and turtlenecks because they think 70-degree weather is cold.

For Barry and his team, going from 38 and a threat of snow to the mid-70's was a treat. Airforce 1 landed safely and soundly in Oahu, even if the President didn't want to fly over because of the fiasco that he met while flying to Toronto.

His inner circle convinced him to fly over rather than his idea of floating over to Hawaii by saying they would never or could never complete this campaign in 50 days if they boated from the mainland to Hawaii.

Barry was happy that his team would be able to spend a day in Hawaii and he felt this was a perfect way to start the campaign as well as giving his team a small, tiny break to enjoy the plushness that Hawaii offers.

Each day included getting up before the sun showed itself and ended around midnight each day. Barry insisted that the team be given at least 2 hours per day to enjoy each state and to venture out on their own. Many of the team members were taking selfies, writing journal entries and really trying to absorb this as much as they could; I mean, when in their lifetimes after this would they have the time and money to go to every single state of the Union?

Day 1- Honolulu, Hawaii

It was now 3 PM and after touring the city's major employment areas and safety departments, Barry had his team venture out onto the main streets of Oahu to talk to residents who may be walking on the sidewalks, enjoying the sun on the beach or having a late lunch or early dinner.

Inside Sura Hawaii on Kapiolani Boulevard, President Whiteman and a few of his team entered the front door. The media was already gathered in front of the restaurant and the owner was given 12-hour notice that the President would be coming.

The Secret Service agents had already secured the area leading up to and inside the building to help make the path inside feel more safe for Barry.

Flashbulbs flickered and Sura Hawaii team members peaked their heads out of the kitchen or the back hallways to get a glimpse of the President.

Bonnie Hallman, owner of Sura Hawaii, came out from the kitchen dressed in a dark olive green dress. She reached out and shook Barry's hands. Barry was wearing a short sleeve button-up shirt, khaki pants and light tan Nike walking shoes as he knew that he would be getting his workout during this trip around the country.

"Welcome Mr. President," Bonnie said. "Would you like something to eat?"

"Well, I thought that I would come to the neighborhood and enjoy some of the finest small businesses in America and I was told by Yelp (he took out his Iphone 7 and held it up) that this is one of the best places to eat while in Hawaii," Barry said smiling.

"We have a booth over here waiting for you and please, let me pay for your meal, Mr. President; it's an honor to have you in my restaurant," she said.

As Barry was walking towards his booth that was reserved for him and a few of his inner circle, he shook hands with people who were sitting in the booths or at stools that leaned up to the bar.

He walked up to a man sitting at the bar who twisted the stool around 90-degrees so that he could see what the commotion was about.

"Good afternoon, my name is Barry, how are you today, sir?" Barry introduced himself to a Caucasian man who was dressed in what looked like clothes that a construction worker would wear.

The man took off his University of Hawaii cap and shook Barry's hand.

"Hello Mr. President," he said.

"Barry, please call me Barry," Barry said and sat down next to the 30-something year old man. "What's your name?"

"Mike, Mike Overtree," he said now blushing as the media and paparazzi was enveloping them as they talked.

"Do you live here in Oahu?" Barry asked.

"Yes sir, born and raised right here, they call us here who were born here, sand babies," Daniel said.

"Sand babies?" Barry started to chuckle. "I don't think I've ever heard that before. Daniel, as you may have heard, my team and I are traveling the country and asking Americans directly what we should be working on.

"We have a ton of money and we have some of the smartest people in the world working with us to help make America better.

"How do you think we should be spending our time and our money to do such an endeavor?" Barry asked.

Without hesitating, Daniel said: "High cost of living here in Hawaii!"

"Wow, you seem pretty emphatic about that Daniel," Barry said.

"Well, sir, I've lived here pretty much my entire life. Like I said, I was born here; but just like the generations before me, my dad, my grandfather, they all worked very hard to make their ends meet, but darn it, sir, for what?" Daniel asked.

"What do you mean?" Barry asked.

"Okay, for example, I am a construction worker. I have helped build most of the newest sky scrapers here in Oahu; I get asked to help out all over the islands and you would think that a construction worker like me, who gets paid very well, would own my own house, be able to travel to the mainland or live more comfortably," said Mike, gripping his cap with both hands.

"But you can't?" Barry asked.

"How can I? I mean, just to get a gallon of milk to feed my daughter, costs me over $5 bucks! I mean, to put clothes on her back almost breaks mine, you know sir?" Mike rhetorically said.

"This is great input Mike," Barry said, writing down in a leather-bound journal that had the Tulalip Tribes logo on the front.

"We work hard, sir. All of us, I mean we all do different things here to make Oahu the magical place it is and to help make the tourists all feel good about coming here and spending their hard earned dollars.

"We just need more help to make our lives just as magical as it is for them sir," Mike concluded.

"Do you mind if we take a selfie together?" Barry asked.

"Really? You want to take a selfie with me?" Mike began to turn red.

"Sure! Are you up for it?" Barry asked again.

The two of them stood up and Barry turned his camera to 'on' and they both got ready for the snapshot. Mike pointed at Barry in the picture as if to say, 'he's the man.'

"Nice pic and nice conversation," Barry said and reached his hand out to shake it. "I've noted what you have said here and will definitely take it to heart. Thank you for your time and thank you for helping to keep Oahu magical for all of us tourists who enjoy coming here with our families."

Barry kept walking deeper into the restaurant, shaking hands and obliging people who wanted to take a selfie with him.

After eating at Sura Hawaii, the team gathered itself up for a 6 PM meeting at the Westin Hawaii hotel. They took up a large ballroom where Jerry and Harmony had the room set up to take notes from each of the cabinet members who also took notes as Barry did.

After a four-hour meeting, the team was excused so that they could get up early the next morning to board Airforce 1 which would take them to the cold weather of Alaska.

After landing in Alaska, the team took to the streets of the city of Sitka. There, they would do the same thing they did in Hawaii and just like in Hawaii, the paparazzi was there as the President walked into local restaurants, shopping centers and the city's only movie theatre.

They met again as a team in the hotel they were staying at to debrief the President as to what they learned in that city.

Next up was Washington State, Barry's home state where they would land at Sea-Tac Airport and from there they boarded their new transportation vehicle that they would spend the next 47-days in.

Each of the 12 commercial buses was fitted for several bunk beds, a few showers and toilets, small refrigerators and stove/microwaves. Each one had 10 or so TV monitors and computers that would link up to each other so that the President could have the debriefs on the road as the traveled from state-to-state.

Before they boarded the busses which were parked on the tarmac, the President briefed the press. He walked up to the podium that had the White House logo on it and behind him was a logo backdrop that had the campaign logo: 50 Days of Enlightenment.

This would be the first press conference he would have on the campaign as he wanted to wait until he had met with more Americans prior to de-briefing America at what he had learned so far.

"Good evening, I'd like to welcome my team to my home state of Washington," Barry said into the microphone. "It's only been a few days since we left the White House to start this mission, this fact-finding mission, and already it has felt like we've been on the road for a week.

"I'm thankful to the residents of Hawaii and Alaska, who were candid with us and have shared with us their stories. How they became a teacher or a librarian, who influenced them and how they have been doing raising their families or struggling to make ends-meet.

"To sum it up, I would say that the campaign is doing exactly what I intended it to do, which is to allow my team, the think tank, the ability to hear first-hand what ills our great country.

"Some of the team members have stated that they have been moved by the stories they are hearing. Some of cried listening to what is affecting our residents.

"We've laughed, we've cried, and we're only at the beginning of this journey. Yet, all along, we're doing this together. We're learning as we go and I am eternally grateful to them for their time and energy; they are truly taking this seriously."

Barry decided before the press conference not to take questions at this time, due to time constraints. He said that he wanted to take time to answer the media's questions right about the halfway point of the campaign.

They got on the bus and exited the tarmac, driving towards Interstate 5 as the skies above, which already looked dark an ominous began to pour with water.

"Wow, looks like we got that press conference in just in the nick of time huh?" Barry said to Ursula who was sitting in the seat next to him.

"How does it feel to be back home Barry?" Ursula asked.

"Feels damn good to be home," he said, looking out his window and overlooking the many buildings and freeway signs in the greater Seattle-Tacoma area.

Barry got on the bus microphone that was linked to the other 11 busses to address the team.

"Okay everyone, welcome to Washington State. On your left, we'll be seeing the beautiful Tacoma dome and on your right, one of my favorite places to gamble, the Emerald Queen Casino," Barry said chuckling into the microphone.

"I'm just kidding, I'm not your tour guide…, but in all seriousness, as you've seen in your itineraries that were emailed to you, we have our first stop up in Puyallup, it's pronounced, 'Pee-AL-up', not 'Pu-wee-AL-up', okay?

"From there, we'll hit the road and make our way down to Vancouver, Washington before we go to Portland and Salem. So, after the meet and greet in Puyallup, we'll reload the busses as you all have been assigned your bunk, enjoy the plushness of the beds, while we get to sleep and drive. How about a round of applause for each of your drivers who will be taking turns at the wheel while we get to enjoy the beautiful scenery of our great country?" Barry said as each of the busses erupted with applause.

Before they left the greater Seattle downtown area towards Puyallup, they stopped at one of Barry's all-time favorite places to eat; Dick's Restaurant.

Barry was flabbergasted that the Secret Service was able to secure the entire block where Dick's on Broadway Street was located.

He got off the bus and was astonished that he could just waltz up to the window and order his meal.

He peaked his head into the opening of the window that separated Dick's team members from the guests.

"Good evening!" Barry exclaimed.

"Uh..uh...hello?" said a 17-year-old African American male who was in his white and orange Dick's uniform. He went to wipe away the sweat from his forehead and knocked off his Dick's paper hat that he was forced to wear as a part of his uniform.

"You okay son?" Barry asked.

"Yeah..yeah..yes sir," the kid responded.

"Okay, then, I'll take a double-double, large fries and a Coke and no cheese on my burger, I got that lactose thing you know?" Barry rhetorically said.

The 12 bus loads of people all indulged in hamburgers, fries, milkshakes, ice cream cones and Barry was in burger-heaven. They loaded up the busses and headed out to Puyallup for the meeting with residents there.

For the next 47 days, Barry and his team stopped at various cities in each state. They listened to the residents, they heard their stories and after it was all said and done, there would be a ton of similar stories, tons of similar ills that he and his team, if they worked hard and worked together could develop a solid work plan.

Barry met with the media for an hour-long press conference when they got to Minnesota. He answered many questions and by then his team was able to get a report ready for not only Barry but, but Congress members who were asking for a report.

Ursula and her team created a website with the URL of 50Days.com that tracked the President's whereabouts and was filled with videos and pictures of residents who raved or just commented normally about this historic trip.

It was now 50 days later and the last city and stop the busses made was in Washington DC, just a few blocks from the White House.

It was now late December, with Christmas just a few days away and Barry and the team wanted to be done with the campaign in time for each of them to spend the holidays with their families that they've been away from for almost 2 months.

They decided to do this stop differently than the rest of the stops where they met with Americans at restaurants, coffee shops, laundry mats and movie theatres.

Instead, they invited DC residents to pack in the Verizon Center for the President to meet one-on-10,000 local residents in a town hall type of forum.

In order for a person to get into this event, they had to show their identification with a Washington DC address on it. The event, which was free, was to allow them to be able to speak freely with the President and no media was allowed to come in.

Barry knew that he was going to get criticized for not allowing the press into the room, however, he agreed with his Chief of Staff who reminded him that all along the journey, the media was only invited to record just a few of the resident's meet and greets.

Inside the Verizon Center, the lights went off and music began to resonate around the entire building. The song Welcome to the Jungle came on and Barry came into the main area as a large spotlight enveloped him.

He already had a microphone on his lapel so he could walk around the arena and answer people's questions. The music slowly faded out and Barry began to speak:

"Good evening Washington DC!!" he exclaimed to the capacity crowd all of them on their feet cheering.

"What a prophetic song to come in on huh?? I love me some Axel Rose and Guns N Roses! Welcome to the Jungle isn't just a song that we wanted to share, but instead it was meant to set a tone for tonight's town hall meeting.

"Life these days are a jungle, and we know that. We heard that all along these last 49 days as we stopped and spoke one-on-one with over 20,000 people over these last 49 states of the union.

"We, I think, heard it all; from the young mother who lives in Austin Texas with her four children, two of them have Austism; to the elderly grandfather who is raising his 11 grandkids because both of his own children are addicted to drugs. We've heard the success stories, of how an addicted mother of 10 kids was able to get through rehab not once, but eight times and then go on to earn her bachelor of arts degree in humanities.

"These are the stories of our people, stories that touch us and remind us of how this great country began. Why my tribal people all around Turtle Island helped the immigrants who came here from England.

"It's our turn now to not only hear from you all but to also compile the information that we gathered and develop programs and services that will bring much needed resources into the homes and lives of our People," Barry said as he started to welt up.

"You know, I come from a long line of leaders, many of whom are no longer with us anymore. Although we grieve today that our leaders are no longer with us, we celebrate the fact that we, all of us in this arena and all of us in America have the ability to help our fellow American.

"How many of us stop when someone is stranded on the side of the road? How many of us speak to our children or the young people of America to share our story with them so that they learn our mistakes for a greater success in their lives?

"We have the capability to help each other, to stop looking at government to be the fix for the ills of our communities. We have the power within all of us to do what we can; to take the time that we know we have to help one another.

"Yes, my dear people, we do! We have that right and we have that power. The power is in your hands and sometimes we let life get in the way for us to remember that," Barry said.

He opened up the floor and one-by-one, there were several questions, several comments and each person was given up to 2 minutes to speak so that it opened up time for as many DC residents as they could.

Three-and-half hours later, the event was over and many people in the audience left there feeling like they were heard or at least their issues were brought up.

Barry and the team piled into the busses and one by one the busses arrived inside the White House parking area where Barry did the best he could to shake everyone's hands or embrace them in a hug.

He went to bed that night knowing that he and his team accomplished something that no other President tried, something that he felt was the right thing to do but he knew this opened up a lot of work for he and his team to get done.

He was exhausted, but he was ready to get these things done.

Chapter 16: With All Due Respect

The following morning, former Republican Candidate Sherry Montgomery and former Democratic candidate Donald Duckson decided to get together for a lunch meeting.

Duckson was already sitting in a booth at a local Village Inn Restaurant in Washington DC, drinking a hot cup of green tea when Sherry arrived.

She plopped her oversized purse down inside the booth and sat down. A server followed her to the booth and immediately asked her if she wanted to order a beverage.

"Two glasses of cranberry please?" Sherry said looking up at the server.

"Two glasses, what's going on, need a flush?" Duckson asked her.

"This damn President is killing me!" she exclaimed.

"You saw his 50 days campaign too huh?" asked Duckson as he continued to read the daily newspaper.

"50 days, 50 states! Who the hell does that?" she rhetorically asked.

"Your President does that ma'dam," Duckson said.

Sherry rolled her eyes and the server got there to deliver her two glasses of cranberry.

They both ordered their lunch and continued to talk.

"So, what are we gonna do?!" Sherry exclaimed.

"About what?" Donaldson asked as he dog eared the newspaper to look at Sherry in her eyes.

"About the Presidency!!! Did you see the latest poll numbers??! HE'S UP OVER 60% NOW!!" she yelled.

"Quiet down now, you'll raise a fuss with the locals here and they are known to talk," Duckson said. "Remember the last time we met I told you that we'll do something to get that red son-of-a-bitch out of the White House in due time? Remember?"

Sherry nodded in agreement. "Well, it's been over a year now since he took that office from us and now we need to-do-some-thing!"

"Impeachment is not an easy job. It's do-able, but not easy," Duckson said.

"Impeachment, is that your end goal here?" Sherry asked.

"What else is there, do you want us to go in there with our hat in our hands and ask that redskin to just resign his post?" Duckson said, slamming the newspaper down on the table.

"I don't care how we get him out of there, let's just get on the offensive, shall we?" Sherry said.

Duckson placed his chin down closer to his neck so that he could look over his reading glasses at Sherry: "I've been doing some research, ma'dam.."

"What did you find out?" Sherry asked taking another gulp of her cranberry juice.

"Some pretty-interesting-things,..." he replied.

"Like?" she asked.

"Like...I've got some incriminating evidence that proves that Barry isn't the boy scout that he makes himself out to be," Duckson said.

"Oh?" she said taking the last gulp of cranberry juice.

The server, who was doing her job too well, was right there as she put the glass back on the table. She stood there and slowly took her time getting the two glasses and Duckson's mug.

"Do you want me to scoot over so that you can be in this meeting with US!?" Sherry yelled at the server.

"I'm sorry ma'am, no, I just wanted to let you know that your food was about to be ready for me to bring to your table," the server replied.

The server turned around and little bits of tears were escaping both eyes.

"You need to calm yourself down and remember that when we impeach that prairie nigger that you and I will be the ones that will get the President and Vice President job!" Duckson warned her. "You must understand that every day is an interview for that job!"

Sherry took three deep breaths and when the server got there with their food, she apologized to her for her outburst.

Duckson began to put all kinds of pepper on his mashed potatoes and turkey meal.

"Looks like you've gained quite a bit of weight there Donald," Sherry said.

"Judging me isn't going to get you the information that I have about your President," he said, slicing his turkey into quarters.

"My President?? Hell, he isn't my President," she replied in disgust.

"Listen, here's what we're going to do," he replied, as he started to butter up his roll. "We're going to continue to do some more research on this clown and gather it all up for us to go into Congress and begin to educate our elected officials about his past.

"Remember, the only ones that can impeach a president are the ones in the House of Representatives and the Senate needs to ratify it, I'm sure they are a little pissed that he's doing this 50-day campaign without them involved."

"I underestimated you Don and I apologize for that," Sherry said. "I'm feeling a whole lot better now that I have food in my stomach."

"Now finish your meal and let's get to work," Duckson said.

Back at the White House, Barry and his inner circle were getting ready for a full debrief session of the 50 Days of Enlightenment that they wanted to get in before Christmas.

Barry already told the entire team that he would be giving them Christmas through New Year's Day off so that they could be with their families.

He wanted one more day with the entire team to get the draft report out to the members of Congress, the media and of course to the American public.

They started at 8 AM and went on until 9 PM that night. They took a few breaks for lunch and dinner but for the most part the meals were a working lunch and a working dinner.

Barry started the session with the same questions that were asked some 55 days earlier and the responses he got back from the Cabinet and other members of the White House team were so much different, so much more in-depth and were backed with so much more credible sources.

Barry could feel the momentum in the room begin to shift towards more energy, more fire and more passion. With each hour that passed, the group began to become more creative and 'blank sheet thinking' began to ensue.

During the dinner break, Barry had a sit down with the inner circle and Yvonne asked him again, what he thought about the information they were getting.

He stood up and said: "I'm pissed!!"

"Again?! You have to be joking Mr. President," Yvonne replied.

"Guess what??...*long pause*... I am!" Barry said and busted out laughing.

The tension that had built up to that moment was released out of there and they all sat back and started to laugh.

"That was not funny, Mr. President," Yvonne said, not laughing but smiling, nonetheless.

"With all due respect, Ma'dam Vice President, I am extremely happy and if I had a happy dance, I'd do it right now... you know, in fact, let's create one right now," Barry said. "Everyone up, off your seat and lets just dance for a few minutes, release all of the energy and see if we can't find ourselves a nice happy dance that we can do over and over again when we succeed."

A few of them didn't stand up and Barry rushed over there and helped them to their feet.

"Harmony, put on some music on your cell phone, let's find some good music to put on," Barry instructed her.

With a few pushes on the screen, Harmony put on the Michael Jackson radio station on Pandora.

Usher's 'Yeah' came on and immediately they all started to find the beat. One-by-one, they were all expressing themselves through dance.

Some were doing the sprinkler, some were doing the hustle, some were doing the running man.

The winner of the happy dance was none other than Yvonne herself, who did what she called the 'shimmy,' where you get into an athletic position, feet should-width apart and you take your shoulders and you shimmy them down to the ground.

Out of breath, Barry yelled out: "There it is! There is our happy dance!!"

They all gathered around Yvonne and created a circle so that they all could see what she was doing.

The door flung open at the sound of the music and there was Carla, with her long camera lense extended from its base.

She began to snap photos of the entire room; people laughing, people smiling and the President himself shimmied down to the ground. He had beads of sweat on his shiny forehead and by the time the song moved onto a much slower one, they were all out of breath.

"Alright! Alright!" Barry exclaimed, as if he was a dance or fitness instructor.

Barry lead the last part of the session and as it ended, he asked the Secretary of Veterans Affairs, Lorrie Laughlin to say a final prayer, which she obliged.

As people were beginning to exit the Boardroom, Barry was there to shake their hands and give them words of gratitude.

The last two people to leave was Ursula and Carla which made Barry a bit uncomfortable.

"Barry, do you mind if I talk to you a little bit?" Ursula asked.

"Sure, Ursula, what's on your mind?" he asked.

"Alone? Can we speak in private sir?" Ursula asked.

Barry and Ursula looked over at Carla who was standing by herself by the board room table.

All of a sudden Carla began to slowly undress by unbuttoning her buttons on her blouse. She gradually walked over to Barry as Ursula came over as well and began to peck Barry on the neck.

The two women began to kiss each other and Barry used both his hands and glided them up and down the backs of both women.

A huge smile flashed across Barry's face as the two women began to kneel in front of him. Ursula began to unbuckle Barry's belt and now Carla had her dress shirt off exposing her large white bra.

"Barry! Barry!" Carla emphatically said, which snapped Barry out of his daydream and back into reality.

"Huh? What?" Barry asked.

"Do you want to meet up after your meeting with Ursula?" Carla asked.

"Oh, sure, that'll be fine," Carla said.

"Very good, I want to discuss a few things with you too before the holiday break," she said and began to exit the room.

Ursula looked at Carla with a very disgusted look on her face as Carla returned the look with a huge smile on her face.

Now that the two of them were alone, Ursula went over and closed the Boardroom door.

"How may I assist you Ursula?" Barry asked.

"Well, I'm not here to see how you can assist me, I'm here to see how I can assist you, Mr. President," she said.

"Assist me?" asked Barry.

"Yes, you see, I know that you are out here in DC and you have no family, I don't know if you have any friends, but I'd like to be your friend," Ursula said as she got into Barry's bubble.

Barry had a mouthful of saliva that got stuck in his throat and he swallowed it. "You want to be my friend?"

"Yes," she said as she began to wrap her arms around Barry's waist. She began to peck Barry's large lips and he allowed her to make him feel good.

It had been a while since he felt a woman touch him. He grew a large erection which Ursula could immediately feel.

"Looks like you feel the same about me huh?" she said as she began to unbuckle his belt.

All of a sudden there was knocking at the door.

"Don't move, don't move a muscle," Ursula instructed him.

She ran over to the door and cracked it open. It was Carla and she knew something was up between her and the President.

"Yes?" Ursula said, looking Carla up and down.

"I really need to talk to Barry," Carla said.

"About?" Ursula asked.

"About none-ya..." Carla said as she placed her hand on her own waist.

"None-ya? What's that?" Ursula asked.

"None-ya business!" Carla replied and bullied her way into the room.

Carla could see Barry's erection through his think black slacks and his belt buckle was still undone.

"Carla! Uh, how can I help.. uh..what are you needing?" Barry said fumbling through his words as he began to buckle his belt back up.

"I guess it's not you that I need huh?" she said as she b-lined to the door.

"Carla! It's not like what it seems!" Barry exclaimed.

Carla turned around. Ursula walked up to Barry: "It isn't? Then what is it then?"

"Uh...um....uh....um..." Barry again fumbled his words.

"Use your words MR. PRES-IDENT!" Ursula said. "Or do you need me to write them for you?"

"No Ursula, that won't be necessary," Barry said in his presidential voice.

Carla went to Barry's left side and Ursula went to his right side. However, Barry was going to answer the next question, would determine who would be happy that he answered and unfortunately, who would be sad.

"You see, I find both of you very, very attractive. I think I would even say that I have found you both attractive from the moment I saw both of you," Barry said. "The fact of the matter is that I like both of you, but I can't have both of you nor do I want that either.

"I've been single for a long time and I have kept it that way for a reason," he said.

"Why Barry? Do you have a low self-esteem?" Ursula asked.

Barry shook his head no.

"Because there's another woman?" Carla asked.

Barry shook his head no again.

"Because you're gay?" Ursula asked.

Barry, one more time, shook his head no.

In unison, both women said: "Then what?"

"I was emotionally hurt by a person of the opposite sex," Barry said, with a big sigh.

"Oh, an old girlfriend from college?" Carla asked as she sat on the boardroom table next to Barry.

Barry shook his head no.

"From high school?" Ursula said and sat down next to Barry on the other side.

"Nope," Barry said looking down.

"Now I'm confused," Ursula said.

"Sally used to live down the block from me and we went out and we had good times and I thought she was my girlfriend, but then she lied and said she wasn't my girlfriend and …."

"Are you talking about back in grade school?" Carla asked.

"You haven't had a girlfriend all these years because you are still upset at what happened when you were like 8?"

"No, not eight….I was 10!" Barry exclaimed.

"10?!" Ursula exclaimed.

"Yes, it hurt me real bad!" Barry said, clutching onto his Sony Notepad.

"I'm out of here," Ursula said, grabbing her briefcase and exited the door.

Carla stayed back and started to rub Barry's back.

"You're not grossed out by this like she was?" Barry asked her.

"It is a bit weird and well… a bit creepy," Carla said. "But, I've went out with weirder and more creepier guys than you before."

"You have?" Barry said.

Carla nodded yes.

"You want to go out with me sometime?" Barry asked.

"Let me think about it," she said.

10 seconds later, Carla replied: "I have thought about it long and hard, and yes, I would love to go out with you."

"Yippee!" Barry shouted out. "Well, I have no friends or family here this holiday and perhaps we can go out tomorrow for brunch?"

Carla replied yes and she pecked him on the cheek, picked up her large camera and walked out of the Boardroom.

Chapter 18: World's Most Eligible

The next morning, the White House front door opened up and in came Carla. "Barry!! Barry! Where are you?"

"He's upstairs ma'am," said Danny, a house servant.

"Is he almost ready?" Carla asked him.

"I'm sure he's getting close, Carla, right?" he asked her.

"Yes, Carla, I think I've seen you around here before?" she asked him.

"Um, no ma'am, this is my first day here," he said as he took a broom and was beginning to sweep up dust on the ground.

"My bad, sorry, I thought I had seen you before," she replied.

She sat down on one of the sofas by the staircase that lead up to the second floor.

She picked up a magazine and began to pretend to read it. About 10 minutes later, she grew impatient. She looked around and saw that no one was around, so she stood up and darted up the staircase towards Barry's room.

Carla entered the living room area just outside Barry's room and began to call for him: "Barry? Are you ready to go?"

She continued to look for him, but he wasn't anywhere to be found in the living room or dining room area. She continued on and went to his bedroom door.

Carla knocked on it and slowly opened the door. "Barry? Are you ready?"

She walked into his bedroom and she could hear him singing in the shower. She sat down next to the bathroom door and began to smile and then laugh.

Barry was singing a Frank Sinatra song:

"I stand as I sway, turn to me, tenderly in the June Night... I stand and I walk, as you look to me in the moon light...a romance, my darling...." The door swung open and a naked Barry pranced out of the bathroom and walked past Carla whom he didn't notice was sitting there.

"A mooooonlight serenade!!!" he exclaimed, his arms stretched to the ceiling, exposing his bushy genitals and his long black hair almost reaching his white butt.

She began to clap: "Bravo! Bravo!"

Her presence startled Barry and he quickly ran back into the restroom.

Carla yelled through the door: "Don't be embarrassed. I'd be more embarrassed with that singing voice than your naked body!"

"Uh..I'll be right out!" he exclaimed through the door.

A minute later, he came out wearing a full plush white robe.

"Your early?" he asked.

"Nope, you're late!" she replied. "Man, why didn't I bring my camera??"

"Thank God you didn't bring your camera," Barry said, using his towel to dry his long black hair.

"I have to say, I did like what I saw..." she said pointing her eyes down below his waist.

"Why thank you, thank you very much,..." he replied.

"That's a sorry Elvis impression," she said.

"A hunka hunka burnin' love..." he began to do the impression again.

"Nope," she said.

"Not even a little bit?" Barry asked.

"You sound like more like Johnny Cash, than Elvis," she said. In her best Elvis voice, she said: "So, why don't you come over here and give this momma some sugar."

She pulled Barry by the ropes of his robe and pulled him in closer to her. She began to kiss him on his lips and began to open up his robe to expose his bare naked body.

He couldn't help but get an erection and just like Ursula did the night before, Carla could immediately tell he was aroused.

"Don't you think we should go out on our date first?" Barry said as he was melting like hot butter with every stroke and every kiss.

"We are on it..." she said in between pecks on his neck.

"Oh, we are?.. carry on..." Barry said and the two of them made their way to the bed. She began to de-robe him and made her way down to his genitals to begin oral sex.

Barry's mind started to wander with all the things that the team and he are going to do after the holidays that no matter what Carla did, especially around his genitals, nothing seemed to arouse him.

"Is it something I am doing or ...not doing?" Carla asked.

"I am so embarrassed," he said and began to put his robe on again and made his way back to the restroom to get ready for the day.

20 minutes later, with a nice relaxed outfit on, he came out of the restroom and saw that Carla was no longer in the room.

Barry went down stairs to see if she was down there and nope, she left.

"Sorry sir, she left about 20 minutes ago," Danny said as he was putting some dishes away in the kitchen.

A few hours later, Barry tried to call Carla but she didn't answer his phone call. He wondered what he needed to do next?

Would she tell others about this? Would he need to get Ursula's help to ensure they were ready for any press questions?

He started to hyperventilate a bit just thinking about what public relations nightmare this could be.

He started to pace around the White House, going back and forth. Barry decided he needed to speak to Carla to ensure that she kept this under wraps.

He called in the only person he knew that could go find her; Paul Elderage, second-in-command of the Secret Service.

"Yes, sir, how may I help you?" Paul said as he walked into the Oval Office.

Barry was sitting at his desk, reviewing some files that he would have to address when Washington DC got back up and running after the holidays.

"Hi Paul, please, have a seat," Barry said, standing up and pointing to one of the seats on a sofa in the Oval Office.

Paul sat down, unbuttoned one of his suit jacket buttons and put his reading glasses on.

"You remember Carla, right?" Barry asked.

"Sure, the photographer?" Paul replied.

"Yes, yes, the photographer. I was hoping you could do me a favor Paul," said Barry.

"Anything, sir, you name it," Paul said.

"Okay, well, I really need to find her, just to speak to her, nothing more and nothing less," Barry assured Paul that there wouldn't be anything more they needed to do, like rough her up or anything like that.

"Okay sir, I'm sure you tried to call her?" Paul asked.

"Of course, of course. When I tried to call her throughout the morning, she wasn't responding to any of my attempts- so..I'm worried..yeah, I'm worried about her Paul; she's a good friend of ours here at the White House and I want to ensure that nothing has gone wrong, you know?" Barry asked.

"Okay, sir, yes, I get it," Paul said, standing up. "I'll have my guys go looking for her, we'll start at the address we have for her and go from there. Is there anything else I may do for you sir?"

Barry stood up too and walked over to Paul: "Nope. That's it, just go get her and bring her right here to me?"

"Absolutely, sir," Paul said and exited the Oval Office.

Barry felt so much better knowing that someone was going to go get Carla so that he could have an understanding with her about what will happen next.

Now that he felt better, he decided to make use of the time alone and go into the White House gym to work out. He put on his exercise clothes and walked-ran downstairs to hit the gym.

He turned on the TV monitors that were in the gym and CNN was on. Barry normally didn't like to watch too much TV, but he thought that this would be a great way to occupy his mind.

Rather than watching the pundits talk about what he and the Congress was and was not doing, he decided to turn the TV to AMC. The movie "BIG" was on and he decided that a good comedy was what was needed at this time.

After being on the treadmill for about 30 minutes, he walked over to the free weights and grabbed a 10 lb. dumbbell. He extended his bicep muscles and retracted them as he watched Tom Hanks maneuver around the big piano to play the song 'Chopsticks.'

Barry smiled and chuckled a bit as he watched the movie. After using the free weights, he decided his exercise time was over. He felt better in the mind and now in the body about the situation he was in.

As he sat in the dry sauna, he couldn't believe how much this issue with Carla had stung him. He could have long days with a ton of meetings about very emotional things like national security, poverty in the inner cities and the like, but he for some reason couldn't shake this issue with Carla.

Perhaps it was because not achieving erection cuts into the man's soul, his identity and his self-esteem. He could make decisions to sign a bill into law and not blink twice, but to have someone else out there that knows that he cannot achieve erection was devastating to his ego.

After showering, Barry went back to his room and he decided to put on some loose fitting clothes, so that he could pray and meditate, then read, then go to bed.

It had now been four hours since the Secret Service had left the White House to go find Carla. Barry thought, how long could it take them to get her? He could've went to her house and been back by now?

Barry decided to call Paul to see what gives. He dialed the phone and Paul did not answer. 'Hmm...that's odd', Barry thought, why wouldn't Paul not answer the phone call coming from the President.

About 20 minutes passed since President Whiteman called Paul, his secret service agent, and finally, the phone rang back; it was Paul.

"Hello, this is Barry," he said.

"Mr. President, sorry I didn't call sooner, but we have Carla," Paul said.

"Yeah, I tried to call you but you didn't answer," Barry said.

"You did?" Paul said.

"Sure, about 20 minutes ago, didn't your phone ring?" asked Barry.

"No, sir it didn't; Carla lives in a weird part of DC, where the phone doesn't get much reception," Paul said.

"That makes sense," Barry said.

"She is claiming that she didn't get any phone calls from you neither, sir," Paul said.

"That makes sense too, okay, so what is your ETA to get here?" Barry asked.

"We're 12 minutes out sir," Paul estimated.

"Okay good, please bring her to the kitchen, I'll be in there having a late supper," Barry said and hung up the phone.

Barry was known for not saying 'see you later,' or 'bye' when ending a conversation on the telephone. It drove Dena and others batty when he didn't say a closing remark and some, including those in Congress he talked to, first thought the President was upset with them.

The fact of the matter is, Barry grew up in an era where the elders of his generation didn't say good bye on the telephone and so of course, he brought that to the White House.

If this issue with Carla was to have happened while he was still living in Tulalip, he probably would've been more passive aggressive about it; you know, he wouldn't bring it up or try to resolve it.

Being the leader of the free world, you have to live a bit on the line, you can't veer from that line or else it has a ripple effect, which causes headaches, more pressure and Barry didn't want none of that.

"You had to have the Secret Service come get me Barry?" Carla said as she entered the White House kitchen. Barry was in there making himself a nice roast beef sandwich, from the leftovers they had for lunch that day.

"Oh, you're here! Great!" Barry said, licking his fingers that had some mayonnaise on them.

"Yes, I am here, what do you want?" Carla asked.

"I want to apologize for what happened earlier today," Barry said, taking his newly created sandwich and sitting at the small table next to a window. Barry ensured they were alone by excusing the kitchen team who periodically enjoyed a nice cup of espresso during the late night hours in the kitchen.

"Apologize for what?" Carla played dumb.

"You know exactly what I am apologizing for," Barry said, taking a big mouthful of the rye bread and roast beef with lettuce.

She waited for him to chew his food and swallow it before she began to talk again: "What happened earlier today will not happen again. I have come to the conclusion that I don't think it's a good idea to date the President. I mean, look at what happened today, instead of you coming to find me, you had the creepy secret service agents crawling around my apartment to find me."

"I had to talk to you Carla," Barry said.

"Right, but if I dated a guy that lived in a regular apartment with a regular job, he would be the one to come over, he would be the one to find me and it wouldn't feel like I was being sent to the Principal's office," Carla said, trying to get comfortable in the wooden chair she was sitting on.

"Look, I've dealt with erectile dysfunction for over 10 years, that's why I haven't dated okay? That was what I was trying to tell you and Ursula earlier today," he confessed.

"Why couldn't you tell me that in private, just before us getting busy like we did?" Carla asked.

"This is a private issue, I couldn't just tell you," Barry said.

"It's a private issue if you were using Rosie Palm and her five sisters to get you off, but I was in the room trying to do that for you and it was very confusing, very frustrating and very upsetting that I wasn't able to do that for you, Barry," she said, almost in tears.

"I know, I know, and I am very sorry Carla, what we did was beautiful and I felt that I wanted to give it a try, but unfortunately for me, I have an issue that I need to take care of and I have been very reluctant to find the solution," Barry said as he stopped eating his sandwich because he was losing his appetite for it.

"Well, I want to help you find the answer to your issue and in the meantime, I have also come to the conclusion that I don't want to date you, okay?" Carla asked.

"I get it, sure, I understand completely; I wouldn't want to date a guy like me that is half broken neither," Barry said, looking down at the table.

She stood up and went over to him: "I'm not dating you because of that, Barry. I am not dating you because of what I said earlier, I want a regular guy that can do regular things like come over when he wants, bring me flowers if he felt compelled; not have the paparazzi with him or secret service agents come find me, that kind of guy."

She half hugged him and he stood up and gave her a full hug.

"Friends?" Barry asked, looking into her eyes.

"Friends!" She said smiling from ear-to-ear.

The next morning, Carla showed up to the White House bright and early. She came in with a file folder with papers inside of it to give to Barry.

Barry was just finishing getting ready for his 9 AM meeting he had with the Secretary of Energy Chris Hamilton inside the Oval Office.

Barry was tucking in his dress shirt when he saw Carla sitting on the sofa outside of his bedroom.

"Carla! Wow, it's great to see you again," Barry said.

"Hi Mr. President, I thought I would stop by and give you some information," she handed him the manila folder with the papers inside it.

He opened it and scanned the documents. "Looks like you've done some research here Carla?" Barry said.

"Yes, like I said, I want to be a good friend, helping a good friend out in his time of need," she replied.

"Very well done and you think the doctors in here would give me the best shot to get the help I need?" Barry asked.

"Yes, I have done a lot of phone calling and emailing of people I know, folks that I have worked with in the past; you know, in photoshoots and stuff. I have a great network of people that I know and the docs on that list are the ones that are the most heavily recommended to work with," she said smiling from ear-to-ear.

"What's in this for you, Carla," Barry asked bluntly.

"Nothing. Absolutely nothing sir, I just want to help you," Carla said. "I mean, you have already done me so much favor just by me being here and having a candid conversation with you; plus, you hired me or at least allowed me to continue with my job here and for that I am grateful."

Later that day, Barry found an hour to go down the list of mental health doctors that would help him achieve his goal of remedying erectile dysfunction. He felt a sense of love and compassion from a new friend, Carla, who said she would not tell a soul about his health issue.

Barry believed Carla when she said that, because it wasn't just the words that came out of her mouth, but the way she said it, so lovingly and supportive.

After speaking to a few doctors, and as he was talking to each of them, he didn't share with them who he was, he finally found one that he felt he could work with.

He asked Jerry to go to the doctor's office and pick up the mental health doctor, Dr. Gary Overton who was shocked to find out that he was going to the White House to 'help an employee there.' Dr. Overton thought that he was going to help a custodian, an assistant or a chef, but not the President of the United States.

Barry was in his living room, outside of his bedroom which would give them full anonymity. They talked for an hour and at the end of the session, Dr. Overton agreed to meet Barry right there every Wednesday to get the assistance Barry needed.

For six straight weeks, Barry was given 2-hour treatment sessions to mentally correct his erectile dysfunction. The final test that Barry had to pass was to have a woman actually get him aroused and to do what average humans do when they are 'in the moment.'

So, guess who he called on to help him with passing the test?

"You want me to do what, Barry?" Carla asked him as they spoke over the phone.

"Yes, it's doctor's orders and I don't want to just go out and get a prostitute, the media would have a field day with me, so please, as a friend, can you just come over and see how I do?" Barry pleaded with Carla.

"This is a bit weird, Barry, you asking me to come over and 'play with you,' to see if you're healed," Carla said. "Well... um....well...okay, but you better not pay me, and this doesn't go any further than just us two, okay?"

A few hours later, Carla arrived to Barry's bedroom. The lights were off and she could see that there was floor lighting so that she could navigate her way around the bedroom without tripping onto something.

"Barry?" she said in a whisper voice.

"Yeah, I'm over here on the bed," Barry whispered back.

"Why are we whispering?" Carla asked.

"I don't know," Barry said in a whisper voice again. "Just come to the bed."

Carla came over to the bed and she could feel Barry's warm body on top of the covers. She reached down and could feel that he was completely in the nude.

"Wow, you don't mess around," she said and began to give him oral sex. "Before I go any further..."

Barry handed her a condom.. "Okay, good, thanks, I was just going to ask for that," she said and opened up the condom and began to fit his penis with it.

An hour later, Barry walked into the hallways of the White House, he was a new man! He began to give everyone high fives and even tickled one of his interns that was bringing garbage to the garbage can.

Whispers and murmurs ran through the White House as everyone wanted to know what got into the President.

'Was he in love?'

'Did he win the lottery?'

'Did he just kill a bunch of aliens and saved the planet?'

Nope, none of that happened, instead, the hard work and effort he put into his mental health sessions worked and he felt more self-esteem, more alive than ever before, and yup, he wanted to start dating.

"Welcome to the Wolfe Blitzer Show here on CNN, my name is Wolfe Blitzer and with me tonight are our two usual advisors, David Satler, former advisor to John McCain and James Blufield, former advisor to John Kerry. Gentleman, thanks so much for being on the show tonight.

"Can you believe what is happening up at the White House? In a statement released by the US Press Secretary, Ursula Tally, the President will be setting up what they call Personal Time Opportunities with certain eligible single women; now is this a ploy to keep the American people talking about this instead of the upcoming National Security Summit or is this legitimate?

"Well, the President is single and has been single for most of his life," Satler said. "He wants to get it on and doesn't want the press to see women tramping in and out of the White House and us thinking they are prostitutes, so I can see why he thought it would be a good idea to just go out and tell people his business."

"I think it's a ploy Wolfe," Blufield said. "The President is getting scrutinized for the ideas that he and his team have about keeping America safe and what better way to get those ideas passed us by talking about lipstick and pantyhose."

Ursula came in and turned off the President's TV in the Oval Office and said: "There, are you satisfied Barry?"

Taking a sip of green tea, Barry stood up and said: "Yup, I am very satisfied. I think its high time that the President be as upfront with what is going on inside the walls of the White House than ever before. I mean, as I date the women that I'm interested in, I can't just go out on the streets of DC and take a love interest out. I have to do my dating here and so I might as well as be upfront and honest about it."

"So now what?" Ursula asked. "You just going to look through Match.com and find a few hot women to bring here?"

"Nope, it's already been set up Urse (he called her Urse, at times he was trying to be more buddy-buddy with her), Carla has given me profile names and pictures of women she knows. I had the secret service run their names for the background checks and everything," he said.

"Carla helped you with this?" she asked.

"Yes, Carla helped me, ...she's helped me out in so many different ways," Barry said looking out into the distance. "You have no idea how she's helped me, she's become a true friend."

"Friend?" Ursula was skeptical. "Friend? Barry...she's in love with you, don't you see it?"

"We've had our discussions and we both believe that not being in a relationship together is a good thing. Friends. That's all we are is friends," Barry assured her.

Date #1

It was a Monday night and the first woman that Barry had over was the one he had the highest hopes for.

Darla Pennington: Single, 32-years-old, Librarian at the Washington DC Public Library. No children, never been married. Enjoys sporting games, long walks, has an affinity for animals and best of all, is part Native American (Navajo).

After eating dinner, the two of them went to the Study to have a night cap. It all came crashing down when Darla got too drunk and began to fall onto all of the furniture and began to throw up all over the carpeting in the Study.

Date #2

A few nights later, Barry's second date had many attributes that he liked about her, but wasn't really his type, physically.

Beth Thompson: Single, 33-years-old, Accountant at a local financial firm. No children, married once but at a young age. Enjoys watching movies, working out and lives a very private life. She is half German and half South African.

Dinner was served and as they began to eat, she couldn't stop laughing. With every bite, she would spit out pieces of meat or hit Barry with mashed potato shrapnel. He didn't know if he was on a date with a beautiful single woman or the comedian Gallagher. She had a nervous tick that made her laugh.

Date #3

A few more days went by, as this was the last date of the week that Carla had set up.

Ginny Ewokiniq: Single. 36-years-old, one child (12), married once, former Miss Universe from Turkey. Enjoys traveling, the outdoors and competed on the TV show Naked and Afraid.

The dinner went extremely well as the two of them had more things in common than they originally thought: they both enjoyed the same types of foods, the same types of movies (comedies, mostly) and were making each other laugh through each course of food that came out of the kitchen.

Unfortunately, the entire thing went south, when after having a nightcap in the newly cleaned Study, as they were about to make love, Ginny had a dirty little secret. She had all the woman parts that most women have, but she also had a man part as well, you get the gist.

Since Naked and Afraid, the TV show, censor the genitalia of the people on their show, if you go back to the episode she was in, the blur lines extended further down from her waist then the rest of the women that have ever been on that show. It freaked out her fellow contestant at first, but the producers cut out the entire 'freaked out' parts.

The White House staffers thanked her for coming and told her that Barry was feeling under the weather.

The phone rang and Barry looked at his cell phone. The caller ID said "Auntie Z" and he pushed the green button on his Iphone 7.

"Nephew, are you there?" Auntie Zeta said.

"I'm here Auntie, how are you?" he said.

"I'm well son, I'm doing just fine, thank you. What are you up to?" she asked.

"I'm just sitting here on my bed, it's been a long week and I'm thankful that it's Friday night," he said in a glum voice.

"You sound sad, what's going on over there?" Auntie Z asked.

"Just another week has gone by, Auntie, that's all," he said.

"Now I hear that you've been dating, son and need I remind you that you are obligated to find yourself a nice *tribal* woman?" she reminded him of a talk-to he had with his late grandmother back when he was 22-years-old.

"I know auntie, but heck, I'm almost 50 and I am not a spring chicken anymore, I may end up with a woman who is not from a tribe," he said, sitting up in his bed.

"Nonsense. Now, there's a woman over here, she's my nurse, she comes over and checks my vitals every Tuesday and nephew, she is the cutest little thing. She's not married, she is dating, but she's not married. She has no kids and I think she's in her early 30's," Auntie Z said.

"Auntie, I don't have time to travel over there right now, but she does sound like a nice woman," he said, yawning.

"You better make time, son. Like you said, you're the one that is getting up there in age and I'm sure you want some woman to play with your little ding-a-ling every-once-in-a-while?" Auntie Z asked.

"Thanks Auntie, (yawning and smiling)..it's about 1 AM over here so I need to get some sleep okay?" Barry said. "Get some rest and I'm happy that you're calling to just say hi and that everything is okay there."

"Yeah, yeah, everything is just fine son. I just want you to be happy and in love. You deserve the best son and you deserve a great woman to be by your side," Auntie Z said.

He hung up the phone and put his head down on the pillow. He started chuckling again at the comments his 92-year-old auntie mom gave him.

'Play with your ding-a-ling'...(chuckle, chuckle).

He fell into a deep sleep.

Chapter 19: From Death to Love

It had been a month since Auntie Z called her nephew in the wee hours of the night. Barry always had a connection with the other side (another term for heaven, the spirit world, etc.) and today he felt something in the pit of stomach telling him that the other side was a calling.

He went about his morning, getting ready, going to the dining room for breakfast, reading the daily paper and it wasn't until he was meditating, just prior to his 10 AM meeting with Vice President Underwood and Secretary of Transportation Victor Rodriguez that the feeling he had grew stronger.

In the midst of meditation, a person goes into a trance. They use breathing techniques that calm the brain down, almost making it still as the night and it's in this trance that some of the most in-depth information comes protruding out of a person's soul.

Auntie Z went to the other side. That was the message that came to him that February morning.

A knock at the door was Dena, his Executive Assistant who had a message for him. The look on her face signaled to Barry that something wasn't right.

"There was a death back at home huh?" Barry asked her.

Dena didn't say a word but handed him the note.

The note was a message from cousin Tammy to call home.

"Hello, Barry?" Tammy said on the other side of the call.

"Yeah, cuzzie, it's me, what's going on?" Barry asked.

"Well, well...it's Auntie Z, she's not doing so well," she said.

"She's alive?" Barry asked.

"Yeah Barry, but the doctors are saying she can go at any time," Tammy said.

"Okay, I'll fuel up and head over there as soon as possible," Barry said, hanging up the phone.

Dena cleared his schedule for the next seven days. He packed his clothes and he along with a few members of his inner circle got onto Airforce 1 and headed out to Washington State.

After five or so hours in the air, they landed safely at Sea-Tac Airport. The media was all set up outside of the Airport, showing images of Barry's stretched Escalade that would take him back to the Tulalip Tribes reservation.

An hour after driving from Sea-Tac, the Escalade pulled up at Auntie Z's house, where she had lived for almost 50 years. Her and Barry's late-Uncle Dominic lived there and raised Tammy and Liz in that same house.

It is customary for Native people to want to die in their own house. Auntie Z was taken from the Everett Medical Center to her house for her to die.

Barry walked into the old, decrepit home and looked around in the living room. He could hear the air ventilator going on and off inside Auntie Z's bedroom. He walked in and saw the tubes up her nose and in her mouth, giving her the air she needed to continue beating her big loving heart.

He walked over to her bed and sat down on a stool that was placed at the headboard of her bed. Auntie Z was alert, having noticing her nephew that she liked to call son, ever since his own parents and brother passed away decades ago.

She couldn't talk, but could only make sounds to the responses that people said to her.

Barry tried for the life of him to stay strong, having spent most of the flight over from DC in prayer, meditation and affirmations, telling himself over-and-over again to not cry, stay strong.

"Hi Auntie!" Barry said, with a big smile, "It's me, Barry. I just landed in Sea-Tac about an hour ago and here I am to be with you."

The air ventilator was very loud and it was already hard enough for Auntie Z to hear anyone even prior to this happening so Barry was speaking extra loudly to her.

Her deep voice was able to muster only deep sounds from her mouth that had the thick plastic tubing pushing oxygen into her listless body.

"I just want to tell you thank you," Barry said as tears started to welt in his eyes. "Thank you for helping me when my parents died. You did a great job and I will be forever in your debt."

Tears started to build up in Auntie Z's eyes and they began to overflow with water, spilling out onto her beautifully wrinkled skin around her big round brown eyes.

He knew she could understand him and emotion overwhelmed him even more. He was filled with gratitude for being there in time to see her final moments, but also feeling the loss that would eventually leave an empty wound in his heart.

He put his head down to her hand and started to cry almost uncontrollably. A minute later, he felt the loving embrace of a few hands that was massaging his back.

He was surprised that someone was touching him and he looked up and saw that it was a woman he didn't know. She was a very beautiful Native woman that had dark brown long hair with highlights in it. She was wearing a stethoscope and a beaded necklace with the Tulalip Tribes logo on it, similar to his signature bolo tie.

Barry wiped off the big alligator tears that was on his face and used his hand, then his hanky that he had in his suit jacket to dry them off.

"You must be Auntie's caretaker?" Barry asked the nurse.

"Yes, you must be her nephew, Mr. President?" she responded.

"She was like another mom to me and ..." tears again started to form in his eyes. "Gosh, I can't stop crying."

She reached out to him and hugged him with a deep loving embrace. She put her hand on his back and used her other hand to stroke his long black hair.

He cried for about 30 seconds on her shoulder and lifted himself from her embrace.

He started to laugh through the tears: "What's your name?"

Smiling from ear-to-ear, she said: "My name is Trina, Trina Smith, I am from our tribe here in Tulalip and it's been a true honor and privilege to take care of your auntie-mom."

Barry chuckled a little bit: "Trina was my mom's name."

"It was?" she asked. "That's pretty darn cool..."

Barry looked down at his Auntie and he could see that she was smiling from the way her eyes formed around the plastic on her face.

He started to smile back at her and Trina asked Barry if he could step outside for them to speak privately. They both went out of Auntie Z's bedroom and she updated him on what was going to happen next. She said that it could be any moment that she would expire and that Comfort Care was on their way to make her last moments on earth very comfortable for her.

Barry nodded and understood what was going to happen. He sat in Auntie Z's room for the next few hours, rejecting anything to drink or to eat. He didn't have an appetite for anything and felt somewhat remorse for being away from the reservation, away from one of his Auntie's who helped raise him.

It was Auntie Z that got Barry off of his pity pot; for a few weeks had gone by after the fatal accident that took the lives of his mom, dad and little brother. Barry wasn't eating and was losing weight rapidly.

His Auntie Z came into his room, opened up all of the curtains and sat down next to him. "Barry, nephew, son, you need to listen to me and listen real good. You need to start eating son, you need to start living again. It was fine to feel the emotions that you have regarding your late family, but it's high tide that you get on with your life."

A young Barry turned over to his other side and put his back to her.

"I know you don't want to hear this from an old lady, but I have to tell you that I was very close with your momma. She was my little sister and it hurts me every day that she's been gone too. I can't call her and ask her to come watch my two little girls. I can't go over to her and ask her for advice on the dress I am going to wear.

"There's so much that I cannot do, son, that it drives me crazy. But guess what? You were not meant to be in that car and I wasn't meant to go down like they did neither.

"We have one life to live and maybe my life's purpose is to see you succeed, maybe God put me here to make sure that I help you go to college, get a good paying job, hell you could be the President of the United States!

"What I can't do, son, what you cannot do, neither, is to give up. You need to get up, take that next step towards your future success and it starts right now. It starts with you getting dressed and into the dining room where your family is gathered waiting for you to eat; waiting for you to move on with your life."

Back at Auntie Z's house, with the last hours remaining of her long life, Barry told nurse Trina that she meant the world to him.

"Yeah, she talked about you every-single-day that I was here. She would yell at the TV when the pundits would criticize you for doing this or not doing that. It would really mess up my work with her because I was here to check her vitals and her blood pressure would shoot up and she would get all flustered," Trina said.

"So, she could go at any time huh?" Barry asked.

Trina nodded yes.

Barry texted Dena to go to Dick's Restaurant and come back with two or three bags of hamburgers, fries and sodas to feed those who were at Auntie Z's.

An hour later, the food arrived and Trina peaked her head into Auntie Z's room where Barry, Charlie and Liz were sitting in her room quietly.

They all sat in the dining room and ate their meal, laughing and telling stories of old times on the reservation and in Auntie Z and Uncle Dominic's home.

Just as they were done laughing about a story at Charlie's expense, Trina came into the living room with 'that look in her eye.'

Barry recognized that look right away, put his hamburger down, swallowed what was left in his mouth and ran into Auntie Z's room.

The entire house went into her room to be with Auntie Z in her final moments. At 10:33 PM on February 12, 2018, Zeta Mary Fryberg passed away.

The family had a wonderful service for their late-matriarch. The entire church was filled with people that Auntie Z met along her journey; people she touched who shared words she shared with them that left their lives better.

Hand drum songs were sung and Catholic singers made the service even more beautiful. Barry was asked to be one of the persons that would walk his late-Auntie's body from the church to her grave.

The media did a great job of staying away from the services with only a helicopter from a distance showing Ariel shots from above.

After the services were over and during the 'dinner' portion of the funeral, Barry could see Trina from a distance, talking with other members of the Tulalip Tribes.

A voice came onto the microphone and it was Mel Smith, tribal chair for the Tulalip Tribes.

"Good afternoon everyone and thank you from the eldest to the youngest for being here for our family's services, my name is Mel and I am the chairman of the Tulalip Tribes. It is my honor to be here with all of you, especially you, Mr. President, during our time of need.

"Auntie Z was always a beacon of hope for us here at Tulalip. She always spent time with us at the council meetings, she would make it here even when she was under the weather and give us her opinion about a decision we the Council was about to make.

"I've been asked by the family to be the speaker for this part of the work and so I'm asking all of her family members to be up here with me so that you can act as runners to thank those who helped make Auntie's services well done."

Barry stood up and walked over to the front where Mel was standing. Mel whispered into Barry's ear that he didn't mean him. Barry put his hand up and nodded as if to say, 'it's okay, I want to be here.'

The family thanked the priest, the choir, the hand drum singers, the funeral director, and finally the cooks.

"We have one more person that we want to give a love offering to, will Trina Smith, please step forward?" Mel asked.

Trina, who was sitting in the back of the auditorium stood up. Mel asked her to step closer to the middle of the floor so that the family could thank her.

"Before we formally thank Trina for her dedication to taking care of Auntie Z before she passed, I have a letter written by our late Auntie that she said she wanted to have read at this moment.

" (in Lashoot-seed) Good day my friends and relatives, if you are hearing this letter, it's because I am now on the other side to be with my family and the love of my life, Dominic.

"I want to thank all of you who have ever been in my life for I couldn't do the work that I do without you. I am so proud of all of my relatives and all of my nieces and nephews. Tammy and Liz, please take care of my home as I love you and am proud of you always.

"To my caretaker, Trina, whom I call 'T', please take care of yourself as you were a great caretaker to me for these many months. I ask you to do me one more favor. Please take care of my nephew, my son, for he needs a woman like you in his life."

Barry's jaw dropped at hearing his deceased auntie-mom leave instructions to Trina. Liz put her hand on her sister Tammy's shoulder and they both started to cry.

Mel's eyes began to water and he couldn't finish reading the letter. "I'm sorry, but this is hard." He mustered up enough strength and continued to read the letter.

"Barry, I want you to go over to Trina right now."

Barry walked over to Trina and waited for her next instructions. Trina was almost in tears as Barry stood next to her.

"Liz, Tammy, there is a blanket that I want you to take right now over to where Barry and Trina are."

Liz and Tammy unraveled a beautiful Pendleton blanket that had the Tulalip Tribes logo on it nice and big.

"I want you to wrap these two people right now."

Liz and Tammy spread the blanket and enveloped the two of them. As they placed the blanket over their shoulders, tears dropped from Trina's eyes.

"I want you two to always stay together, let this blanket remind you of the love I have for you and that I am always going to be with the both of you, hugging you and giving you strength. I love the both of you and will always be here."

Trina took one end of the blanket with her right hand and Barry took the other with his left hand. They were now wrapped in a blanket, a symbolic gesture to show love, unity and in the traditional ways, this was a sign that they were married, ..Indian-married.

The men with the hand drums started to pound their drum sticks on the drums and started to sing a beautiful honor song. A friendship circle formed and the somber moments turned into a celebration. A few minutes later the song ended and each person came up and shook their hands or gave them a hug.

Chapter 20: A New Life

Barry went back to DC without Trina not because he didn't find her attractive, or that he didn't think they could be a successful couple, but he knew that he had a lot of work to do back east.

He quite frankly, wasn't sure if he could be in a successful relationship and be President of the United States. All of the long hours, the traveling; could a relationship form despite all of that plus the added pressures of making gigantic decisions that could affect the entire planet?

Were these feelings of not having a relationship true or was he just feeling depressed from just burying the person who helped shape him into the man that he is today?

A year had gone by since the funeral and it was coming up on the end of his second year as President and many of the programs that he started which were based on the feedback he got from the 50 Days of Enlightenment were about to begin.

He wanted to make sure that he was in touch with the Directors of each of the programs and services that he went to bat for. He knew that if done correctly, that these new programs could vastly benefit those who really needed it.

He met with the program directors via Skype once a week for the first 100 days of their launch. After that, he met with them monthly and then gradually he would hear from his Cabinet once a quarter about each of their successes and failures, which they all learned from.

Now that a year had passed by he could now have the time and foresight to see past the work he and his team were doing.

He hadn't talked to Trina since he left Tulalip and it was starting to show up in his life. He began to feel a sense of loneliness and on top of that a little regret for not doing what his late Auntie Mom wanted for him, which was to be with Trina. To pass the time, Barry decided to take the offers that had always be there to do a few out-of-the-ordinary things.

For example, Jimmy Fallon asked him to go on his show several times, and now he decided to do it. He was featured on a "THANK YOU NOTES" segment of the show which was one of the highest rated shows in the history of The Tonight Show.

The producers of The Walking Dead extended an invitation to have him on the show as a 'walker' which he finally said yes. In one scene, Daryl is outside of the White House and a herd of walkers surrounds him and he ends up stabbing Barry in the skull and kills him instantly.

After his scene was done being filmed, he walked into the green room, where only he was allowed to be in (for security purposes).

As he walked inside, he could smell a strong odor coming from the back of the room. Looking up at the lights on the ceiling, he noticed a thin white smoke; it was smoke coming from someone toking on marijuana.

"Who the hell is smoking...!" Barry said as he walked around the corner of the locker area. Former Presidents Bill Clinton and George W. Bush were sitting on a few Director's Chairs lighting up a blunt.

"Oh, hey, Mr. President...how was filming?" Clinton asked.

"Hey guys, it went well, what the heck are you up to?" Barry asked.

"What's it look like?" Bush said. "We're smokin' in the boys room!" Bush started singing the iconic song with Clinton laughing beside him.

All three of them laughed and Barry decided to sit next to them.

Clinton took a puff and tried to pass it over to Barry. Barry rejected the offer by putting his hand up.

"Well, how things goin' rookie?" Bush asked Barry.

"Pretty darn well, Mr. President, I have to say, they are going well," Barry said.

"When you going to get a Mrs. President, Mr. President?" Clinton asked.

"There is a gal that I have my eye on but.." Barry said.

"But, what?" Bush asked.

"I don't know if I can handle being the President *and* being in a relationship," Barry said.

"You know Barry, I've been married to Mrs. Bush for over 30 years and sure, we were married before we moved to the White House, but you get in the groove of things, you know?" Bush said, chuckling.

"You don't know if you have time to be in a relationship and run the country? Hell, look at what I did..I had time for Hillary and for God-knows-who.." Clinton said taking another big toke from the marijuana filled cigar.

Bush broke out in laughter: "You got that right, boy!"

"I got into everything, didn't I?" Clinton said giving Bush a tap in his side with his elbow.

"You were open more than 7-11, Bill!" Bush exclaimed.

"Hell, I didn't know when to stop. My nickname was the energizer bunny," Clinton said. "Don't believe me? Look at this tat I got recently to remind myself of the good-ol-days.." Clinton said as he lifted up his dress shirt to reveal a pink energizer bunny on his side of his abdomen.

"So, who you pokin' now son?" Bush asked Barry.

"Well.., no one George, why?" Barry asked.

"Why??" Clinton asked.

"Why??" Bush repeated Clinton because he wanted to know too.

"If you ain't gettin' no tail as the leader of the free world, you are vastly disappointing me son," Clinton said taking a small toke and passing it over to Bush.

A producer of The Walking Dead came in and told the two former Presidents that they would be filming in a few minutes.

They both stood up and told Barry that they had to leave. "It was a pleasure to meet you son, I hope that you have more luck with the ladies than you do now!" Bush said.

Barry stood up too and shook their hands. The two former Presidents exited the green room, with Clinton's left arm over Bush's shoulder blades and they left the room laughing about something.

Barry was on the cover of Time Magazine for being the world's most eligible bachelor. When Trina saw that edition on the newsstand in downtown Seattle, she was a bit upset at reading that headline.

For Barry, he felt that it was going to be a new life for him. Now that he understood what had been ailing him the past 30 years, he felt confident that he would find love and would do anything he needed to do to get in love and keep it.

That's the beauty of a new life, you get to start over.

A new life is also what former Republican Candidate Sherry Montgomery wanted for herself. She finally decided to enter herself into a WA DC treatment center to help her cope with her alcohol addiction. The Presidential campaign really took a lot out of her and she used alcohol to cope with the loss of her bid to be President.

She had given up hope that she would be President and the more she thought about the idea of trying to oust President Whiteman, the more she just wanted to close this chapter of her book of life. A big part of her counseling was to remove the demons in her life and through that process of dealing with her demons, she was able to remove many fears: fear of spiders, fear of trees, fear of failure.

When Donald Duckson met her outside the doors of the treatment center on her last day, she didn't know how she was going to tell him that she didn't want the Presidency anymore. She practiced what she was going to say in the mirror in her room prior to leaving the treatment center.

"Donald...." she paused. "Donald...." Looking away from the mirror. She made a fist and put her right hand up as if to say 'put up your dukes': "Donald, I am a lover, not a fighter....no that won't work."

She practiced several different versions of what she was
going to say to Donald.

Finally, when it was the moment of truth, she told Donald:
"I'm out. I don't want to screw him over and I don't want to
be apart of this..this...plan that you've probably conjured
up," she said with her chest puffed out.

"Wow, treatment cleaned your mind up too huh?" Donald
said.

"I have just had some time to think about it and yes, one day
I would love to be the President, but not like this," she said
shaking her head.

"Even if I have some dirt on the guy?" Donald said with a
half-smile.
"Even if you had a Ram truck bed filled with ...filled
with..well, what dirt?" she asked.

"I knew you'd want to know, get into the car and I'll tell you
all about it," he said as he put his hand on the bottom of her
back and opened the car door to let her in.

Back at the White House, Barry was getting ready to see
Trina for the first time since they laid his auntie Zeta to rest.
Even though he felt that he could go on a dating spree, there
was something there between he and Trina. Barry thought it
was time to find out so he called her up and asked her if she
would meet him in DC.

She had been playing a bit coy with him since the funeral, but
on Barry's third attempt to get her to come out there, she

finally said yes.

He was having a bugger of a time figuring out what to wear. Finally, he just decided to put on some jeans and a Seattle Seahawks t-shirt.

Trina was due at Reagan National Airport anytime and she was going to take an Uber from the airport to the White House. Barry offered to have one of his team members pick her up, but she said she wasn't his wife or his girlfriend and that she wanted to go on this trip on her own.

Her reason for saying yes to the trip to Washington DC was to see if she could be around Barry even though he was the Commander in Chief. She did have feelings for him but she wanted to also find out if those were true feelings or was she just in awe that he was the President of the United States.

She wanted to tour DC to see if she would even like living out there but don't underestimate her, she knew how to put one foot in front of the other.

The White House doorbell rang and the Secret Service agent nearest the door, alerted Barry that Trina was on the front porch and that it was safe to open it.

Barry opened the door and saw a cute, petite woman standing on the porch. Trina was wearing a large parka, thick gloves and ear muffs to along with her blue jeans and boots.

She did a little dance, tapping her toe and her heel.
"I'm here!" she exclaimed.

"Yes, you are!" Barry said. "C'mon on in, it's freezing out there."

Trina came in and Barry offered to take her carry-on suitcase and her coat.

"Wow, you pack light," he said.

"I'm only here for a week and besides, you said that there was not going to be any big fancy events this week, so I only packed the bare minimums," she said.

"May I show you to your room ma'dam?" Barry asked and bowed like a servant.

She curtsied and said: "Yes, my captain, please show me the way." Looking around the White House she said: "Nice place."

The two of them walked up the staircase and went down the hallway that lead to Barry's room. Trina had studied the White House map online and noticed that this was the similar direction to his bedroom.

"Uh, you are putting me in a different bedroom, that's not yours, correct?" she confirmed.

Barry stopped and turned around: "Nope, I'm keeping you in my room and tying you up."

Her face turned from light brown to red in 0.5 seconds.

"I'm kidding, I'm kidding, no I am putting you in a bedroom just a few doors down from mine," he said. "I don't want to put you in that wing over there and the wing on the other side of that is closed."

"Closed, what happened?" she asked.

"I taped it off," he replied.

"Taped it off?" she asked.

"Yup, I used tape and I made it so that no one can go through there," he said and put his right hand up. "This whole place was way too big and it's just me here, plus I couldn't ever find anyone in this big house."

"Tough pill to swallow," she replied.

"I don't get it," he said.

"Nevermind, how about showing me where I can get my jammies on?" she asked.

"Oh, yes, let's continue on," he said.

They both continued down the long hallway until Barry came to a door that was closed.

"That looks like it has my name on the door," Trina said pointing up to a gold plated nametag that was eye-level to her.

"I was going to have them put a star on the door, but I thought that would be a bit too much," he said.

"I think the name tag is a bit too much, but I think you were trying to send a message?" Trina asked.

"Yup, that this is your bedroom and you will always have it here as long as I live here," he said.

Trina entered the room and the entire room looked and felt exactly like her room back in Marysville, WA. Barry had a designer get pictures of her bedroom and created the exact replica to help make her feel more 'at home' there inside the White House.

"Oh my God! Are you serious Barry?" she said, as she put her hands over her mouth. "It looks just like my bedroom!!"

She toured the entire room and picked up the same pictures of her as a child, her same dresser drawer, the same...everything, down to the teddy bear that an old boyfriend won at the Puyallup Fair.

"You even have Chuckles here?" she said as she picked up her teddy bear.

"Uh, yeah, we had a difficult time finding that stuffed animal," Barry said smiling.

"If this is your way of trying to court me, you won!" she said.

"I aim to please," Barry said. "I'll get out of your hair, but don't go to sleep, please? I have arranged for our first date downstairs in the dining room," he said.

She nodded and Barry left her bedroom.

20 minutes later, as Barry was sitting at the dining room table, the fireplace beamed an orange light and the smell of cedar was wafting through the White House. The lights were down and there were a few plates of freshly baked cookies, almond milk and napkins were placed on one end of the dining room table.

"Barry?" a small voice could be heard in the distance.

"I'm in here, Trina," Barry yelled out.

She came in wearing a pink robe, her hair was in curlers and she had on pink bunny rabbit slippers.
"Nice getup," Barry commented to her.

"I figured that since you re-created my bedroom for me, that I would show you what I'd be doing in that room right now had I not took a 5-hour flight to get here," she said and sat down at the table.

"Makes sense," Barry said grinning.

"What's all this?" she asked, then after a small hesitation she got it. "Oh, this was what your Auntie used to make you for your birthday?"

"Yup, I wasn't like the other kids who wanted a nice cake and ice cream," he said picking up a cookie. "I was a simple kid, who wanted simple things."

She picked up a warm chocolate chip cookie: "So, are you saying you're still a person who like things simple?" she asked.

He bit into the cookie and said: "Yes, I do. I'm just an old fashion Indian from the rez."

They sat and enjoyed the cookies and talked well into night and into the early morning.

They talked about lost loves in their past, they talked about what they wanted in the future. They both wanted to get married, they both wanted children and they both wanted to be happy with someone; grow old with that person.

As much as Barry wanted to keep the momentum of the time that the two of them had the night before, the next morning, while in bed, he received a text from Chief of Staff Harmony that the Cabinet wanted to get back together for an emergency meeting.

Barry rushed around and got showered and put on a nice tan and blue suit. He wore his usual Tulalip Tribes bolo tie and brushed out his hair.

He asked the kitchen to just make him a simple egg and sausage burrito which he took and walked into the Oval Office.

"What's goin' on?" Barry asked Harmony.

"Well sir, the Cabinet members felt that we needed to get a meeting together this morning regarding Columbia," she said.

For the past year, one of Barry's work plan deliverables was to curb the drug epidemic that had been plaguing America. This was one of the 'asks' that the team received during their 50 Days of Enlightenment tour that they did a while back.

"According to Secretary of Defense Granger, he said now is the time to strike in Columbia sir," Harmony said.

"Why now?" he asked.

"I'll let him explain it to you better, but in a nutshell, the Columbians are having their elections and if we want to make a deal or if we want to do an imminent strike against them, now would be the time," Harmony said, as she placed a three-ring binder in front of Barry who was sitting behind his desk.

Barry studied the information that was prepared for him. An hour later, with binder in hand, he walked into the Executive Boardroom. The entire Cabinet was already there and they all stood up to greet him.

"Alright, everyone have a seat, now let's get to business," Barry said, taking off his suit jacket. "In reviewing the recommendations of this body, it looks like the three options are to: (a) do nothing and continue to monitor Columbia (b) send Secretary of State Youngman there to broker a deal or (c) use lethal force?"

"Yes, sir, those are the three options we have and..." said Granger.

Barry interrupted him: "Ashton, I don't see any reason for us to use force at this time, please explain to me why this was in the recommendations?"

"Well, sir, I think using force is always something we need to consider," he said.

"Consider? Consider going in there and risking American's lives?" Barry asked.

"Sure, sir, I mean, we need to send a message," Granger said.

Barry who had already rolled up his shirt sleeves used his hands to communicate his points: "The message is peace, Ashton; if we want peace to this issue then we must go in with peace in our hearts. I don't want us to start a war with Columbia unless we ultimately have to."

The entire Cabinet began to murmur words to each other and Barry had to settle them down.

"I'll open up the floor to you all to share your ideas," Barry said, sipping his ice water.

"We're losing this war on drugs," Secretary of Health and Human Services Borenstein said. "As you can see in tab 4, the drug epidemic has spread so far and so wide that now we're seeing 10-year-olds addicted to heroin. 10 year olds!!! These are our babies and more and more of them are trying it for the first time and overdosing on it. WE MUST DO SOMETHING!" she said, with a slight tear in her eye.

"When I first got on this team, back in the Bush II administration, drugs were a topic, but not a focus," said Homeland Security Secretary Ian Ettman. "It's a crying shame how much this has been an issue, I have a cousin and a brother who both OD'd on heroin in the past few years."

"Dropouts are at an all-time high, Mr. President," said Secretary of Education Moses Everman. "Either they are dropping out or their test scores are so low that it was like the kids were never there. We've pinpointed heroin as the main culprit for the decline in our education system."

"Although there are other countries that supply the heroin and cocaine that comes into our country, we must go directly to the one country that supplies the most, which is Columbia," said Granger.

The Cabinet all shared their ideas and input with the President. After the four-and-a-half hour emergency Cabinet meeting, the President decided that rather than go in with peace and to try and strike a deal, imminent force was going to be the first attempt to making the Columbians stop harvesting and importing opium poppy, which is the main ingredient in heroin.

That night, while eating dinner with Trina, the President was very quiet.

"Are you okay Barry?" Trina asked Barry who was slouching in his chair, somewhat playing with his food. "You haven't said much this entire time."

Barry perked up a bit, not trying to show the fear that had developed in the pit of his stomach after directing his team to use force towards the Columbians.

"How about after dinner, we go into the theatre and watch a movie?" Barry asked.

"Theatre? You have a movie theatre here?" Trina said smiling.

"Yup, and we have all of the movies, even the ones that are in the theatres all around the Nation," Barry said, placing his fork down on his plate.

Barry didn't eat much but wanted to take his mind off of the eventual war versus Columbia. Watching movies was always a nice get-away from his problems. Some people use alcohol, drugs or sex, Barry used comedic movies to take his mind off of things.

The two of them walked into the small movie theatre, with a big bucket of popcorn and two extra large movie cups with soda inside each of them. She had with her a box of M and M's and Barry had a large package of red vines.

"Wow, this place is packed," Trina joked with Barry.

"Yeah, I don't know if we can find a seat," Barry went along with the joke.

They stepped into the middle row and sat down in the middle seats, placing them right in the middle of the large movie screen.

The lights dimmed and the movie began.

"Say Anything?" Trina said chewing the last remains of the popcorn she placed in her mouth. "Really? A movie that takes place in the Seattle area?"

"I LOVE this movie," Barry said as he took a big twig off of the red vine that was in his hand.

The scene where the two main characters were in the car making love signaled Trina to place her head on Barry's chest. She leaned back into him and they both watched the movie.

He placed his right hand on her forearm and she reached up and began to slightly touch his hand, flirting with him. She looked up at him as the glow of the movie drenched over his face.

She reached up and began to kiss Barry, first on his thick lips and then his chin and then his neck. He sat up, which forced her to sit up. He began to kiss her on the neck as he placed his hands down the sides of her body. Barry reached down and began to take her shirt off.

Trina was wearing a pink bra which covered her voluptuous breasts and was above her toned abdomen. She reached over and took his shirt off and began to kiss him on his chest and back up to his neck.

He reached around her and took off her pink bra and her breasts gently fell onto his stomach. Just as the moment was going to take them into eternity, the theatre lights came on and two men came rushing into their private space.

"Sir!" said one of the secret service agents. "Sir, we need you in the War Room immediately."

They were both startled and Trina, not having enough time to retrieve her shirt that Barry threw four rows behind them just covered her chest by cuddling closer to Barry.

Barry stood up and kept Trina on his chest so that the agents couldn't see her naked upper body.

"Okay, get out of here, I'll be right in," Barry said angrily. The two men left the theatre and Barry looked down at Trina.

"I-AM-SOOOO-Sorry!" Barry said. He gave her a peck on the cheek, grabbed his shirt, went four rows back and threw her shirt over to Trina and darted out of the theatre.

Inside the war room, Secretary of Defense Granger, Admiral Davis and a few others were there waiting the President's arrival. They all stood up as Barry, who was still in his casual wear sat down.

"What is so important that you needed to interrupt me during my flex time?" Barry asked.

"Sorry, sir, we tried to text you but it looks like you may not have had your cell on you," Granger said. "It's the Columbians, sir, they must have been tipped off to our plan, they took a few Americans hostage and sent us this video."

The war room lights dimmed and Granger placed the mouse on the video clip and double clicked it. The video showed two Americans, both blindfolded at first and then the armed gunman took off the blindfolds. It was a man and what may have been his wife.

The woman started to cry as she said exactly what they wanted her to say: "My name is Violet Moore and this is my husband Earl, we were here on a mission to help underprivileged Columbian children when we were taken from the village. Now they say that unless America backs down from their plan to invade Columbia, they will shoot us and take more American hostages until they get what they want."

Just as she finished that sentence, a machine gun is shown inside the video 'scene' and the armed gunman pulled the trigger, firing multiple bullets into Earl, killing him instantly.

Violet plunged onto her husband's dead, limp body, screaming and crying as blood gushed all over the room and onto her.

The video ended and the lights came back on. "Now you see why we needed to talk to you, sir, they are going to kill more of our people if we don't back down," Granger said. "How shall we proceed?"

They went back and forth, talking about how their plan of attack was leaked and how quickly that leaked out to the Columbians.

Finally, after an hour of discussion, the President said: "Well, it looks like the only option now is for me to go over and sit with President Gonzales there in Columbia."

"Are you sure we want to do that?" Granger asked.

"Yes, I think the only way out of this now is to go over and try and talk some sense into him," Barry said.

Chapter 21: Keepin' the Peace

The next morning, Barry had breakfast served in Trina's bedroom. She awoke to the clamoring of glassware and dishes being carted in. She sat up in her bed and stretched.

"This is courtesy of the President who had to leave on a peace mission, he sends his love and hopes you have an amazing day today," said the head concierge Paul who they all called Pauley.

There were plates of pancakes, waffles, crepes, fruit bowls, hot oatmeal, salmon potato hash, wheat bread an assortment of juices and coffee. Trina plunged into each of the foods with a gigantic smile on her face.

Airforce 1 landed in Bogota Columbia, where armored vehicles came and picked up President Whiteman, Granger and Ettman. Barry didn't want a large group of them going into hostile territory and even ensured that Vice President Yvonne Underwood stayed back at the White House under protective custody.

The armored vehicle stopped at the security gate where President Hernan Gonzales lived and after giving their credentials, the gate opened up to allow them in.

President Whiteman got out of the vehicle and was met by President Gonzales who promptly shook Barry's hand. The two of them walked into Gonzales's mansion and proceeded to the lawn on the other side of the building.

It was a gorgeous 74-degree day, blue sky, birds chirping in the background and President Whiteman believed that they would walk out of there with a peace agreement signed and that both sides would get what they needed.

Two chairs and a small table set between the chairs were placed on the lawn for the two of them to sit and enjoy some coffee, wine or other spirits of their choice.

After sitting down, they began to speak openly about their situations. President Gonzales first speaking to the importance that the products produced by his country, including opiates had on his country's economy.

"Our poppy fields produce 50% of the revenue that my country needs to sustain itself, President Whiteman," Gonzales said. "There's no way in hell that I am going to allow my fields to stop growing revenue that we use to feed, protect and nourish ourselves with."

"Before we get into the crux of why we are here, Mr. President, I want to tell you a bit about me," Barry said.

"I know all about your, Mr. President; you and I are a lot alike," he replied. "We both come from modest means, both were elevated into prominent positions, even at a young age, and we both believe in doing what's right for our people."

"Wow, it looks like you've done your homework about me," Barry said. "Even though you may have done some research, I wanted you to try some things that I believe you will enjoy; each of the following items that I brought with me, come from my reservation back in the United States."

"The things you are sharing with me, was checked by my guys right?" Gonzales asked.

Barry shrugging his shoulders and putting his hands out as if to say 'heeeyyy, what do you take me for?' said: "Of course, Mr. President and the things I am giving you, I will try first, so that it will ease your mind?"

President Gonzales nodded his head yes and the presentation began.

The first item that Barry wanted to share was a package filled with smoked salmon, directly from Barry's homeland, Tulalip. Barry took a pinch of the smoked salmon and placed it on his tongue to show President Gonzales that it was safe to eat.

"See? Now you try it.." Barry said to President Gonzales.

President Gonzales looked at the smoked salmon with a lot of focus, eye balling every aspect of it. He bent down a bit to smell it and it passed the sniff test. He took his right hand and with his first finger and thumb, he took a eeeny teeny pinch of salmon.

"C'mon, try a bigger piece, you won't regret it," Barry said smiling big and his eyes even bigger.

President Gonzales took a bigger pinch and then placed it above his face.

"Yeah, go ahead, put it in your mouth," Barry said as he watched the Columbian President slowly place it in his mouth and begin to chew. Gonzales's eyes got wide and a smile replaced the stern look he was giving Barry.

"This is esta buena mi amigo!!" (translated, 'this is good my friend') President Gonzales said.

Barry began to talk about the drug epidemic even more to President Gonzales. He spoke about the overdoses that was happening all over the United States and in record numbers.

The more Barry talked, the more President Gonzales took from the smoked salmon love offering. By the time Barry was pausing from speaking so much about the history and effect of drugs in America, especially in Indian Country, 95% of the smoked salmon was gone and in President Gonzales's belly.

"Mas! Mas!" President Gonzales shouted. "But wait, what about the fish head?"

"Oh, that's the best part my friend," Barry said and pinched out one of the smoked salmon's eyeballs and popped it in his mouth.

President Gonzales cringed at the sight of Barry eating a fish eyeball.

Chewing the eyeball like gum, Barry said: "C'mon, now your turn, eat the other one."

President Gonzales put his pinchers out above the fish head, looked up at Barry as if to say 'seriously?', pinched the remaining eyeball out and popped it in his mouth without hesitating.

Gonzales began to chew it and chew it and his eyes began to water. After about the 10th chew or bite, Gonzales spit out the fish eyeball.

"Oh, well, I guess the eyeball isn't for everyone," Barry said, shrugging his shoulders. President Gonzales took out a silk hankie from his back pocket and wiped his mouth off which had some saliva on it.

"The next thing we'd like to offer you is some refreshing cedar tea," Barry said, taking a thick wine glass full of it from Ettman. President Gonzales took his from Ettman and immediately smelled inside the crystal glass.

Barry, just as he did with the smoked salmon, took a gulp of it to show President Gonzales that it was okay to drink.

Seeing Barry take the gulp, President Gonzales did the same thing and filled his mouth with the iced tea-looking beverage.

"This was made from my homeland, at Tulalip," Barry explained.

"Tu-tu...tulay-..?" President Gonzales was trying to say Barry's tribe's name.

"Yup, Tu-lay-lip," Barry sounded it out for him.

Closely watching Barry's lips President Gonzales said: "Tu-lay-lip.. ahhhh...Tu-lay-lip...si, si...I didn't quite know how to say your homeland, but thank you for teaching me that."

"The elders say that the cedar tea is healing medicine against cancer, against evil spirits and many of our family members back at home make this from beautiful cedar trees that surround our territory," Barry said. "Every time I drink cedar tree, I am re-energized and filled with hope and happiness."

Gonzales took another swig of the cold beverage and nodded his head yes.

"So, Mr. President, we come to you in peace. We come here to talk to one another rather than fight one another," Barry said, placing his cedar tea drink down on the small table next to them.

"The final item that we want to share with you is what we call a peace pipe," Barry said. "Now, it isn't as customary for my people at Tulalip to smoke from the peace pipe, this is more of something that we would see with the Plains Indians or other tribes from the South."

Barry was handed a beautifully handcrafted peace pipe made of stones of the Acoma tribe in New Mexico. It was carefully placed in a leather along with a stunning turquoise beaded leather pouch which had Washington State grown marijuana, laced with a secret ingredient inside it.

"Just like the Standing Rock Sioux Tribe who came to the White House to ask for help with a proposed pipeline, you and I will smoke from a peace pipe and there will be no lies between us," Barry said holding the peace pipe up.

Barry opened up the pouch and took a pinch of marijuana from it and placed it into the 'bowl' of the pipe. He packed it pretty good as President Gonzales was watching every second of the presentation.

A secret service agent came over and placed a beautifully beaded lighter in President Whiteman's hand. Barry took the peace pipe in between his lips and lit the bowl.

White smoke came out of the pipe immediately and Barry took small puffs from the pipe into his mouth and released the smoke quickly.

Gonzales instantly had a big smile on his face as he could smell the marijuana burning from Barry's mouth and from the bowl of peace pipe.

"Gon-jah?" President Gonzales asked. "That smells like marijuana!"

"Yup, grown inside my home state of Washington," Barry said proudly.

President Gonzales pretty much stole the peace pipe from Barry's hands and lit that puppy up. His eyes began to water as he took a deep breath of the peace pipe.

Barry began to speak: "Even though we ask of you to remove the opioid poppy fields that you have here, we will pay for the cost of removing it and give your country $3.4 million per month to cover the revenue that your country normally gets from selling it to illegal drug makers in my country."

Barry had to hurry up and get to the point because laced inside the marijuana was a few grams of peyote, which he was told would take into effect in less than 4 minutes after inhaling it.

President Gonzales, upon hearing how much his country would be getting over a billion Columbian pesos per month from the United States, smiled extremely hard, almost looking like Cheech from Cheech and Chong, nodding his head and taking another toke.

"To get this started, we have drafted up some papers that indicate that your country will cease growing poppy fields and burn what is currently there," Barry said, handing President Gonzales a clipboard with a signature line for President Gonzales to sign.

"You know, Mr. President?" Gonzales said. "This has to be the happiest day of my life. I believe that this is a win-win for both of us, your country and mine. So, I am signing this agreement to keep peace with our countries and to know that I have a friend in you."

Water began to fill in President Gonzales's eyes as he signed the document. Barry took the signed documents and gave them to Granger who placed them into a locked briefcase and put the briefcase in a vault inside the vehicle that transported them to Gonzales's house.

"You got any more of that smoked salmon?" asked Gonzales.

Barry took another package out of the box next to him which had another entire smoked salmon inside it. Together they began to pinch off meat from the bones.

Just as President Gonzales was pinching another thick juicy chunk of smoked salmon, he looked at the fish's eyes and they began to pop out at him.

"Adios mio!" President Gonzales stood up. "El pez esta vivo! El pez esta vivo!! Como puede ser! Como puede ser!"

Translated, he said: "The fish is alive! The fish is alive! How can that be?! How can that be?!"

He shook President Whiteman's hand and bolted back into his casa, locked the doors and went to bed.

"Guess he can't handle the good stuff huh Ashton?" Barry asked him. He began to walk towards the armored vehicle when Barry stopped in his tracks.

"Do you hear that Ashton?" Barry asked him.

"Hear what sir?" Granger replied.

"That noise...it sounds like someone asking for help, shhhhh...do you hear that?" Barry asked again.

"Uh, no sir, I don't, I'm sorry.." Granger said.

Barry looked down at his hand which had the smoked salmon and he slowly opened the packaging around it. As he opened the packaging, the voice got louder.

"You see! That fish is alive! It's asking me to help it!!" Barry said and he threw the smoked salmon on the ground and ran towards the armored car. The secret service agents took out their guns as a few of them escorted Barry back to the cars and a few stayed back and slowly examined the smoked salmon.

Granger walked up to the secret service agents who were studying the remains of the smoked salmon.

"Don't worry boys, that fish is indeed dead, the two Presidents were having a trip-out session from the peace pipe they smoked," Granger said.

That night, Barry walked into the White House west wing entrance, directly off the helicopter that brought him back from Airforce 1.

Sitting on the couch next to the bottom stairs of the staircase was Trina, dressed in a plush white robe. Her dark skin and newly made hairdo accompanied her big smile and red lipstick.

"Welcome home Mr. President," Trina said in her best Marilyn Monroe voice.

Barry drug himself through the White House as he was extremely exhausted from the long flight home. Untying his bolo tie, he said: "Oh, Trina, I'm so happy you are here."

"Oh?" Trina playfully said. "Why's that?"

"You are the rose amongst all the thorns of this world," Barry said as he reached down and hugged her. He followed this up with a big kiss on her thick voluptuous lips. "I wonder if you can help me find something in my bedroom?"

"What would that be Mr. President?" she innocently asked.

Grabbing her by the hand he escorted her up a few stairs: "You'll see."

The next afternoon, the Cabinet gathered again to get a full update from Barry about the peace making trip to Columbia. Barry told them about flight, about the food and yes, about the agreement that President Gonzales signed.

The entire Cabinet room erupted in celebration from hearing that Barry got Gonzales to sign the document, thus ending the supply of harmful opioids from at least one country.

"Breaking news right here on CNN, the President is about to give a Presidential update on some news in the fight against drugs," Wolfe Blitzer said which interrupted the news that he was already giving. "We'll go now to the East Lawn of the White House, where President Whiteman is now exiting the White House towards the podium."

Barry slowly walked towards the podium, almost marching towards it and put his two hands on it and began to speak into the microphone.

"Today, is a beautiful day that the Creator has given us. We stand on the shoulders of giants, many of whom have given it their all to help us in the fight against harmful drug addictions that have plagued this country for far too long.

"Today, marks a victorious day, for all recovering drug addicts, for our children who deserve to live in a country that is free from all that harms them, and for our elders who have prayed relentlessly that we, the United States do something to protect our children from illegal drugs.

"Just yesterday, Columbian President Gonzales and I met in his beautiful country where we shared cultural items, we ate smoked salmon and drank cedar tea.

"We also shared in a document by signing it which now ends the growing of poppy fields that supply illegal drug makers the necessary ingredient that makes heroin and other drugs so powerful.

"Today, we took back our right to live in a society where people can get high from life, not from needles, pipes or makeshift plastic pipes.

"Yes, it will cost America $3.2 million per month or over $43 million a year to keep Columbian farmers from making the drug that we estimate kills over a million people per year.

"The $43 million annually is a small price to pay for American lives and we are ecstatic that President Gonzales and I have a mutual agreement and understanding for both our constituents."

After a few closing statements, Barry turned around and marched back into the White House.

"There you have it, President Whiteman giving us an update on a little trip he took to Columbia where he just gave the fight against drugs a swift uppercut blow to the chin," Wolfe Blitzer said. "With us are our normal political contributors David Satler and James Blufield, gentlemen, what do you think of the update that the President just gave us?"

"I'm blown away Wolfe," Blufield immediately said. "What an idea to go into one of the biggest growers of opioid poppy fields, flash some US money and walk out of there without having to use force. This President continues to shock me on how smart, how astute and how for a lack of a better word, Presidential he has become in less than 4 years."

"Satler, do you have anything to say?" Wolfe asked.

Satler shook his head no.

"Okay, there you have it, one contributor who is raving about the news and the other who is left speechless," Wolfe said.

Chapter 22: The Hail Mary Pass

"Can you believe that son-of-a-bitch did it?" Donald Duckson said to Sherry, whom both were sitting in Donald's dining room area watching Fox News.

"Did you see his latest poll numbers? They're through the roof," Donald continued. "The American people cannot get enough of him and of course he did his little tour of the late night shows, he threw the coin toss at the Superbowl, we have got to do something now!"

"I told you, I am not for this anymore Donald, I don't even know why I'm here?" Sherry said, sipping on her green tea.

"Because, as I have already told you, we have a lot of work to do to get that son-of-a-bitch out of the White House. We can't continue to allow a Redskin to be commander in chief," Donald said, as he poured himself a glass of scotch.

"Really Donald? Now? It's only 11 AM?" Sherry said grabbing her coat and gloves.

Donald ran over to her and grabbed her elbow. Sherry looked down at his aggressive gesture and pulled her elbow away from him.

"Look, I'm sorry, I'll pour it out, but Sherry, I need you to help me through this," Donald said, pleading with her.

"To do what?" she asked.

"I need you to go into the White House and ask Barry a few questions about his past," he said.

"His past? Why would he ever talk to me about his past?" asked Sherry.

"Because you are going to pretend that you are struggling with 'coming out' as a gay woman," Donald proposed.

Sherry, spitting out her green tea said: "What??!"

"Yup, you are going to be mic'd up and you are going to get the President to admit that he's gay," he said.

"But, Barry isn't gay Donald," she replied.

"That's not the dirt that I really got," Donald said. "I know I told you that he may have had a fling or two in his first months as President, but that's not the real dirt."

"Why did you lie to me?" she asked.

"I needed to see if you could be trusted with information that I was going to give you," he replied.

"So, you want me to go in there and pretend that I am a person who needs advice about coming out?" she asked.

"Exactly," he replied.

"I don't know Donald, who is your source?" she asked.

"Let's just say that we did some sniffing around back on his homelands and overwhelmingly that is what most people who 'are in the know' (he said using air quotes) told my guys about him," he said.

"So, he admits he's gay then what?" she asked.

"Duh, we leak it out to the media and let them have a field day with it," he said.

"What will that do?" asked Sherry.

He went over and escorted her to the couch and sat her down. "Listen, the American public was okay with electing a black President; they were okay with a woman nominee for President, but the American public will not be okay with having a fairy as a President."

"I'm listening," she said.

"All you have to do, is pretend that you are going through this life crisis and get him to say he is gay and bam, we got him!" he exclaimed.

Sherry reluctantly agreed to get wired up and after she confirmed a meeting with the President, she went to the White House.

Barry met her just inside the Oval Office by giving her a handshake. She knew he was a hugger so she took his hand that he had put out for a handshake and brought him in closer for a hug.

"Come on in, have a seat," Barry said and closed the door behind her.

They both sat down on the couch and Barry could see that she was visibly upset.

"What's going on Sherry?" Barry asked.

Looking down and twiddling her thumbs, she looked up with weepy eyes and said: "Barry, I know I haven't been the nicest person to you as I agree that I have said some downright nasty things about you, about your people and where you come from."

Barry nodded his head and took a deep breath.

"So, I really am here to apologize to you for all that I have done wrong," a tear dropped from Sherry's right eye. She really was telling the truth.

"Come on Sherry, don't get too weepy on me now," Donald said as he listened in on the conversation.

"I've gone through treatment, Barry, to help me uncover something that has bothered me for quite some time," she said. "I had been having these thoughts about stuff."

"Like what?" Barry asked.

"You know, stuff..." she said standing up. She went to the window and looked out. She continued: "As a little girl, I absolutely loved Shirley Temple. I thought she was the most talented and cutest little girl in the world. Mae West? Ooooh...don't get me started," she began to touch herself around her own genitals.

Barry unloosened his bolo tie and poured himself a glass of water sitting on the coffee table in front of him.

"The kicker was when I saw that scene where the dress of Marilyn Monroe flips up in the wind? Remember that?" she asked.

"Huh?" Barry was lost in the moment.

She sat down next to Barry and said: "So, as you can see Barry, I have had these thoughts and I don't know how to handle them.

"I want to be who I am and I want the world to know that I am well... well...." She paused. "Do you know what I mean?"

"I know exactly what you mean!" Barry said standing up.

"Ah ha! Here we go, we got that son-of-a-bitch," Donald exclaimed in the van that was parked a few blocks away from the White House.

Barry continued: "I had this uncle of mine, back on the rez, who was revered for being a leader, he was a church leader, he enjoyed arranging things for the elders, for all intense and purposes, he was a man of the people.

"Then one day, he lost it; his mind that is, and decided to take his own life because he couldn't bring himself to tell the community that he was gay," Barry said, sitting back down on the couch. "Is that what you're trying to say?"

"Well, well..." she replied.

"Go ahead Sherry, you can tell me," Barry assured her.

"I'll tell if you do?" she said.

"If I tell you what Sherry?" Barry asked.

"That story about your uncle wasn't true was it? That story was about you huh?" she said nodding yes with her big eyes wide open.

Barry stood up and put his hands on his hips. "NO! I really meant that, I had an uncle who killed himself because he was too proud to come out of the closet."

Sherry stood up: "I'm so sorry for your loss Barry, and I'm sorry for thinking that you are gay."

"I have nothing but love for people who choose life partners that are the same gender, but I love women Sherry," he said smiling in disbelief.

Sherry started to gather her things and made her way to the Oval Office door. "I'm so embarrassed, I'll see myself out."

She opened the door and bolted out of there leaving Barry in disbelief. He found it a bit funny, actually but he chose not to follow her out of the White House.

Sherry spoke into the microphone: "I'm going to kill you Donald."

Sherry got in the back of the van that Donald was staking out in. As she got into the van, chuckling, Donald said: "Well that blew up in our faces didn't it?"

Sherry's face was beat red: "I'm so embarrassed Donald! I can't believe you conned me into doing that!"

She opened up her blouse and exposed her bra and the wire that was attached to her sternum. She ripped off the wire and threw it at Donald.

Shielding himself from getting whiplashed Donald turned his back to her for a second. "Now, now, there's more dirt on the President."

"How many times do I need to tell you, I'm out!" She exclaimed. "I don't want nothing to do with this anymore. The only good thing that came out of that was that I told him I was sorry for the mean things I said to him during the campaign trail. So, for the opportunity to make amends with him will never be forgotten, even if it meant my impending embarrassment."

"Don't worry, I'm sure that story won't leave the Oval Office," Donald said to try and calm her down.

"It better not; and *you* better not tell a soul neither!" she said.

A few weeks had gone by since Barry was accused of being gay and upon thinking about that, Barry felt at ease with it all. He knew he had been single for quite some time, he had never been married.

There was no prior history of a break up so some people could think he was gay. Those who don't know Indians very well may have just assumed he liked men because he kept his hair nice and long.

He loved women; he always had and he always will. Barry's problem was that he was normally too shy, or too conservative. Some of his friends growing up would tell him that he put the vagina on a pedestal or that he had too much respect for women.

Most women would say that you could never have too much respect for women; but if you look at Barry's history with women, up to the point that Trina came into his life, you could see that he probably did truly respect women way too much.

For example, back in college at Western Washington University, his freshman year in the dorms, Barry was somewhat seeing a woman from Oregon.

She would come over to his dorm and they would have study time together, watch a movie and cuddle. When it came to the 'moment of truth', even if the woman was spending the night, he never made the first move.

He felt that if he did that, she would scream rape or worse off, not tell him she was violated and then report it to the police.

Another example was later in life, as the President of the National Congress of American Indians, he and a bunch of friends went out to a steak dinner in Washington, DC.

Afterwards, a chairwoman from the 29 Palms Band and he continued from dinner onto a nightcap. They ended up talking about life and love until the wee hours of the night.

They ended up sleeping on the same bed, but she was under the covers and he was on top of them. He never made a single 'move' towards her.

How was he going to be with Trina on this issue? Would he continue to put that vagina up on a pedestal? His first few moves he made, including the night they made love, he had veered away from that line of thinking and was more aggressive.

Trina only packed for one week's worth of clothes, but since things were going great between her and the President, she decided to stay longer. It had now been a month since she arrived to the White House and both of them were really feeling comfortable with the whole situation.

Sure, there were times when Trina didn't see Barry because he worked from sun up to dawn on some occasions. A few times she went to see him in his bedroom but he was sound asleep.

Sherry and Donald tried a Hail Mary pass in the end zone and failed miserably. Barry decided that he too would throw a Hail Mary pass but he felt that he would not only catch the ball but win the game.

It was now the spring, and the National Congress of American Indians were having their spring meetings in San Diego, CA. Barry convinced the Cabinet that he would want to be the first President to attend the gathering of tribal leaders. He said it would be great to get his base all energized again and he would be able to hear from the tribes themselves on what issues are affecting Indian Country.

He decided to take Trina along with him as it would be the first time they would travel together. This would be another test between them to see if they really did have feelings for each other or was it just in private?

Airforce 1 landed at San Diego International Airport and most of the streets from the airport to the Convention Center were shut down to accommodate Barry and those who would accompany him to the conference.

As the stretched Escalade approached the Convention Center, about 1,000 tribal leaders and their team members were all gathered at the entrance to see Barry pull in.

Secret service agents swarmed the front of the building and secured it for Barry's safe passage in. As he walked in, Trina was right by him and a barrage of paparazzi camera people flashed their cameras with each step he took.

Barry shook hands with tribal leaders as he walked in. Many of the onlookers wondered who the woman was with him.

Everett Buchanon, tribal chairman of the Sycuan Band of Kummeyaay Indians was the acting National Congress of American Indians President, the same role that Barry had before he was asked to run for Vice President with John Dungberry. He was standing just outside of the ballroom where Barry would give the opening speech of the entire conference.

"Mr. President!" Buchanon said, reaching out his right hand to give Barry a handshake.

"Mr. President..." Barry replied.

"It's absolutely a pleasure and honor to have you join us for the conference," Buchanon said.

"I'm only able to be here until late tomorrow afternoon and I'll be heading back out of here," Barry said.

"We'll take any time that you have, sir," Buchanon said. Barry was escorted back into a make-shift green room that he and his team would occupy while they were there. On the wall was Barry's itinerary of where and when he needed to be at certain places throughout the large convention space.

Looking at the itinerary, Barry said: "Wow, looks like the same issues, the same set up that we've always had for NCAI huh?"

"Yup, I don't know if we'll ever change that format," Buchanon said. "As you can see there, sir, you go up on stage in about 15 minutes. Now who is this fine young lady you have with you Mr. President?"

"Barry. Please, call me Barry. And next to me is the fine and intelligent Ms. Trina Smith. She is a Tulalip just like I am," Barry said.

Trina extended her hand and Buchanon shook it using both of his hands. "It's truly an honor to meet you young lady," he said.

Trina nodded in response to Buchanon.

"I'd also like to welcome you to our home territory here in San Diego," Buchanon said.

"Why thank you, and please send our gratitude back home to your people for always opening it up for this convention," Barry said as he took a seat on a stool that was next to the door leading out into the ballroom. He began to roll his sleeves up as he continued to talk.

"I decided that I wanted to come back and listen to the leadership. I want to be the first President to take the wish list of the tribes and really accomplish every single one that we are able to do," Barry said.

"I have every confidence that under your direction and leadership, we can actually fix some things in the amount of time you have; which by the way is how long?" Buchanon asked. "Another four years after this term?"

Barry smiling from ear-to-ear looked down and said: "Hold your horses Mr. President, let's just get through this convention okay?"

On stage, Buchanon was introducing Barry to the capacity crowd that gathered in the General Assembly meeting. For every tribal leader there was at least one team member next to him or her; whether that be a lobbyist or an attorney. The Navajos for having over 100,000 enrolled tribal members had three attorneys and four lobbyists with their tribal chairwoman.

Barry was introduced and the entire audience stood up and cheered their current and former leader. He waved his hands as if to say, 'everyone calm down.'

"Enough..! Enough!...please everyone take your seats!" Barry said over the clapping and cheering. The leadership stood and clapped for over 2 minutes with chants coming from the audience: "Four More Years! Four More Years!"

"Alright, really, everyone please have a seat, we have a lot to go over," Barry said. Finally, every person who had a seat sat down as more and more tribal leaders were trying to inch their way into the gigantic ballroom.

"When I was thrusted into this position, I really didn't know what I was doing. Being the person responsible for the hundreds of millions of people is daunting for any person who has had the blessing of being President of the United States of America.

"In the 2.5 years I've been in the White House, I feel that I've seen it all. I think I've aged 10 years since I took that oath of honor and I want to take this time to apologize to all of you for waiting this long to come and talk to you.

"I'm here to listen. I have with me the greatest team assembled on earth to take copious notes and to see to it that we make every effort to accomplish the goals that need to be finished for the sake of all tribal members," Barry said to a rush of applause by the capacity crowd.

"Before I get off the stage and turn my mouth off and my ears on, I want to tell you a few things that I just signed this morning while on Airforce 1 that directly affect all of you today," he said as the entire crowd quieted down to a mouse peep.

"First of all, I just signed a petition of pardon for Leonard Peltier...and..." Barry tried to continue to speak but the entire audience erupted as if he just told them that they all won a million dollars. Tribal leaders were hugging each other, some were crying.

After a minute of pandemonium, many of the ones in the room shushed the other members of the room to allow Barry to continue.

"It's been far too long for our elder to be put in jail, as of 10:04 AM this morning, he is a free man!"

After another minute of clapping, cheering and hugging, Barry continued.

"Furthermore, as you recently heard, the United States made an agreement with Columbia for them to end their harvesting of poppy fields which will only slow down the onset of illegal drugs in America. This act of peace will not end addiction in America, but if we make it harder for the addicted to get their drugs, then I think we slow down the overdoses, the first-time drug users and we do all of us a favor!

"I have signed into law, a new policy that will affect each and every one of you. To my left, on stage, I have my Secretary of Homeland Security Ian Ettman, who also endorsed this new policy. Beginning June 1st of this year, every tribe will be getting Homeland Security money to put up a border, if they so choose, which will make it harder for those who have illegal drugs on their person to come into the borders of our great tribal nations. This bill includes money for drug sniffing dogs, hardware and software to make tribes more intelligent in allowing only those who wish to do no harm to our addicted, our elders and especially our children!"

The entire crowd bursted into applause again and it took another 2 minutes to calm the frenzy down.

"I have one more piece of legislative news and then one personal note I'd like to share with you. Also, on Airforce 1 this morning, yeah, I was a busy man as I made the five-hour flight over here. I just signed into law a bill that will honor all of the treaties that were signed back in the mid-to-late 1800's that should've been kept throughout history. One of the major parts of each treaty is education and that as an exchange for the land and water, islands and mountains, education and health care would be given to all enrolled tribal members. That promise has never been kept...until now. Beginning June 1st of this year, all enrolled tribal members will have free education and free health care!!" Barry said as again, the entire audience was beside themselves, many were crying tears of joy.

Five minutes later, the crowd settled down from hearing all of this amazing news.

"Finally, the rumors are true ladies and gentleman, I am in love!" Barry said smiling like a little boy scout. "I have brought with me a woman that I absolutely enjoy being around. She is my best friend, she is my partner and we go back to her days as a caretaker for my late auntie-mom who passed away. Her dying wish was to have me marry this woman one day and today, I would like to honor my late-auntie mom's wishes.

"Trina Smith? Where is Trina?" Barry asked. Trina's little frame came out of the trees that were standing on the stage next to her and she had her hand over her smile.

"This little woman, a Tulalip just like me, is someone I can see myself growing old with. Now, I was going to wait until we got back to DC to ask her a question, but you know what, I would rather do this in front of all of you, my extended family," Barry said as he walked up to Trina and knelt on one knee.

"Trina Marie Smith, will you do me the honor of being my wife, my partner for life, my first lady and marry me?"

Without hesitation, Trina screamed: "YES!!!!" She immediately started crying tears of joy. The entire crowd went bezerk.

Twitter, Facebook and Instagram all shut down as the majority of users were sharing all of the news up to and including the President's proposal.

CNN, Fox News and all of the local and regional channels had a hard time keeping up with the news that was coming out of San Diego. Most of them were focusing on the marriage proposal and some of them focused on the hundreds of millions of dollars that was just allocated to spend on tribal members health care and education.

For the next 36 hours, Barry and his team did a great job of attending meetings, listening to land, gaming, economic development, water and other issues that each tribe faced.

In a statement written by the President's office, Barry wrote to each tribal leader that he was honored and humbled with the new information that he received from each of them and invited them all back for an update on each of them in six months at the White House.

Chapter 23: Four More Years?

Barry had a little over one more year left in his and Yvonne's term as President and Vice President of the United States.

He didn't get too involved in the work that Yvonne set out to do which mainly consisted of advocating for women and children's programs and services.

Barry's inner circle wanted to find out what he wanted to do in the future: run for a second term or duck out. So, they decided to put it on the agenda for their Monday morning meeting.

"I see that you guys have a question for me to answer on this morning's agenda?" Barry asked the small group consisting of: Yvonne (Vice President), Harmony (Chief of Staff), Jerry (Executive Assistant), Ursula (Press Secretary) and now Trina, who is set to be the First Lady in six months.

"They want to know for their own sake what they should be gearing up for Mr. President," Trina said.

"I see, I see…you want to know whether or not I should run for President again? Let me think about this for a minute," Barry said.

"We need to know this week, Barry, if we want to start a new campaign," said Harmony. "The Republicans and the Democrats are already set to name their candidates for the upcoming election and we need to know if we will be too?"

"I apologize for the tardiness of this as it's been pretty crazy here with all the work we're doing to finish up the promises we made from the 50 days' campaign and now the tribal priorities we announced a few months ago at NCAI," Barry said.

"That's okay, Mr. President, if you give us the green light this week, we'll be on track for the election," Ursula said.

"I think I'll call around to my family at home, I'll sit with my fiancé and we'll give you all an answer on Wednesday?" Barry said.

The meeting continued and they adjourned a few hours later.

"Breaking News tonight out of Washington DC, I'm Janice Thompson, in for Wolfe Blitzer. US President Barry Whiteman has just announced he will run for President next November as he seeks his second term.

"Let's go right now to Pennsylvania as President Whiteman was there attending an American Cancer Society fundraiser...."

"I did a lot of soul searching, I talked with my fiancé Trina, my family back in Washington State and I have come to the conclusion that our work is not done yet."

Thompson continued: "Democratic Party Candidate Donald Duckson has been confirmed as that party's number one nominee and Texas Governor David Peterson just got the Republican party nod for their Presidential candidate.

"Stay with us all year long as we continue to see how the election develops right here on CNN."

Barry's phone rang and on the other line was former President Barack Obama.

"Good evening Mr. President," Barry said as he answered the phone.

"Good evening to you Mr. President," Obama said. "It is great to hear that you are seeking a second term. I just want to tell you that it warms mine and Michelle's heart to know that you are going to be on the ballot; your leadership-your guidance through tough times has been a blessing. I wish you and Trina nothing but success next November."

"I stand on the shoulders of giants, and you Mr. President, have always been a giant in my eyes. I accept your congratulation remarks and I will be calling you more than I have in the past as we hopefully embark on the second term of the work you started and that I and my team will finish," Barry said.

Barry had just hung up the phone as his car pulled up in front of the Thomas Waterman Estates, a five-diamond hotel that he was staying at in Pennsylvania.

The door opened and the secret servicemen surrounded Barry as they escorted him in. There were about 30 or so cameras there to record Barry walking into the hotel, many reporters who were screaming out questions about his re-election bid as the rain poured down from the East Coast skies.

Barry looked left and was smiling at the cameras when all of a sudden a burst of flames was seen in the closeness of the crowd and Barry felt a sharp pain in his neck.

"The President's been shot!" someone yelled out in the crowd.

The gunman walked closer to Barry and was yelling out: "No demon Injun is going to run my country! Be dead injun, be dead Redskin!"

The secret service agents mauled the gunman, by first taking the gun away and then dog piling on top of him. One of the agents alerted the rest of the team by radioing in a Code Joker, which meant the President was shot, bring medical help immediately.

Barry was on the ground, blood squirting out of his neck. The rain was washing the blood away from his neck as soon as it came out. All he could hear was a loud ringing in his ear drums and all he could see was people looking down at him with rain drops pouring into his eyes.

Six minutes later, four ambulances showed up and all of the paramedics swarmed the President, each wanting to quickly do their jobs and save Barry's life.

One of the secret service agents, a former paramedic, was able to sustain the gunshot enough for the true paramedics and all of their tools and medicine to arrive.

The next few hours would be crucial for the doctors at the Pittsburgh Medical Hospital and the country lie dormant as they awaited the verdict of whether or not Barry would survive the surgery.

Inside the hospital, Barry lay in the Intensive Care Unit. His lifeless body hooked up to tubes and machines that beeped. A mask was over his mouth pumping oxygen into it.

The doctors did the best they could to release the pressure that the wound to his neck had on the rest of his body. They were able to take the bullet out and patch up the vein in his neck that was causing some internal bleeding.

Barry would have a scar on his neck that if he lived through this incident, he could laugh and tell his future children about.

A few days had gone by and since Barry had lost so much blood, he became unconscious; some of the medical team believed that it was possible that he went into some sort of shock that caused his brain to shut down.

Trina, Uncle Jack, Aunt Georgianna and Liz all made the trip to Pittsburgh to see Barry, with Trina being picked up last by Airforce 1.

Eventually, many tribal leaders from all around the Nation also came by the hospital to try and show their love and support. Outside of the White House, there were many signs saying things like "Get Well Mr. President", "Speedy Recovery" and other messages.

Trina entered his hospital room where she saw the love of her life surrounded by wires and tubes. She began to cry and just held his hand, watching the oxygen pump into his chest.

She sat down next to him and began to pray. As a nurse, she would see patients like this during her time at Everett Memorial Hospital yet, nothing ever prepares a person to see their loved one like that.

Trina was a practicing Catholic and she did what her family and friends at the local church taught her to do, which was to say an 'Our Father' and 10 'Hail Mary' prayers.

She was deep into her prayer when she heard a knock at the door. It was Uncle Jack who came in first followed by Liz and then Auntie Georgianna.

"How's my nephew?" Uncle Jack said with a very concerned look on his face.

"The doctors say he's got some sort of brain shock issue that has caused him to stay unconscious," Trina said. "The actual wound on his neck, where the bullets went, is doing just fine, but it's his brain that is needing rest."

"What the hell we supposed to do for him?" Auntie Georgianna said rather loudly.

"The doctors said all we can do now is just continue to talk to him, ask him to come out of it," Trina replied. "I just don't like to see him like this."

Liz came over to her and gave her a big hug. She asked her if she ate anything and Trina shook her head no. A few minutes later, Liz came back with some soup and a sandwich for Trina.

Every hour, Trina would ask the family to gather around Barry's hospital bed and form a small circle to say some prayers. After saying some prayers, they all began to talk about their lives, sports, issues affecting Tulalip and the country; anything to keep him hearing them.

At first it was a bit weird to talk to someone that wasn't conscious, but as they say, it's only weird if it doesn't work.

That third night, waiting for Barry to awake, Trina fell asleep on the chair next to the bed. Just as she was in a deep sleep, Barry began to come to.

He opened his eyes and saw Trina curled up in a ball on the chair. He began to speak to her but as loud as he was, she wasn't moving.

"She can't hear you," said a man dressed in all black. He had wavy dark black hair, a mustache and go-tee.

"Who are you?" Barry asked the man.

"Who do you think I am?" he replied.

254

Barry sitting up in his bed looked at him even closer.

"Oh my God, are you Prince?" Barry asked.

The unknown man nodded his head yes.

"I thought you were…wait a minute…does this mean that I'm dead too?" Barry asked him.

Prince shrugged his shoulders and said: "You're a good man Barry."

"Thanks man, I try to be a good man, I try to do what's right," Barry said. "So, if I'm not really awake, how the hell do I get awake. I mean look at that woman right there."

"Oh your fiancé?" Prince asked. "Heck yeah, I'd get awake for that woman any day of the week. So, what are you waiting for?"

"I guess there's a part of me that doesn't want to go back, does that make sense?" Barry asked.

"No, explain?" Prince said.

"Well, it's like all of this, I mean, if I wake up, the entire world will be up my ass with a camera all asking me this or that question," Barry said tugging on one of the wires that lead to the machine that beeps.

"Do you know what I would give to have one more minute on earth and you're crying around because you are bothered by the paparazzi and people who love you?" Prince asked. "Get the hell out of here man."

"It's not that, ….well, I guess it is kinda like that," Barry said. He paused and looked around a bit more. "Wow, that purse over there looks like my Aunt G's purse, is she here too?"

Prince nodded yes.

"Hmm..it would be great to see my Aunt and anyone else that is here," Barry said.

Prince began to sing "When Dove's Cry" in acapella. Barry sat there and just listened to him sing the verse. Prince got to the chorus and as he was about to sing the second verse, Barry woke up from his coma.

Sitting next to the bed, holding his hand was Trina. She was in deep meditation, breathing in and out as deeply as she could to calm her nerves down.

Squeezing her hand he said: "Fancy meeting you here young lady, come here often?"

"Barry! Oh my God, Thank YOU God, (she looked up to the sky) Thank you God for bringing him back to us!" Trina said kissing his hand. "Look who else is here honey, Auntie G, Liz and Uncle Jack."

"Hey son, looks like you wanted to come back to us after all huh?" Uncle Jack said, holding Barry's other hand.

Auntie G stood up and started singing and dancing: "Daddy's home...daddy's home...ohhh..daddy's home...

"Hey son, so happy to see you back up, how are you feeling?"

Smiling from ear-to-ear, Barry said: "Oh, my head hurts, feels like I got bonked in the head or that I have a hangover or something."

Surgeon Gavin came in just as Barry said that and came to his bed. "Well, look who decided to join the party. How are you feeling Mr. President?"

Barry at first didn't say much to the doctor, his medicines that were being sent into his veins numbed him to pain and to the present.

It wasn't the medicines that were causing a cat to grab his tongue, it was more about the fear that resonated inside of him. He was fearful that he was going to be told some bad news like he was paralyzed or that he was going to die.

"Oh, that's okay, Mr. President, the stuff we gave you will all wear off pretty soon," the doctor said as he stood next to Barry's bed looking down at him. "Our prognosis is that we'll be monitoring you every hour, just to be safe and to ensure that your body is progressing the way it needs to.

"In reviewing your X-rays, I can see that the bullets, yes, two bullets, not just one, didn't do as much harm or at least long-term harm to you as it could have.

"One bullet went directly through your neck and the other one was lodged in there pretty good. We were able to sew both sides of your neck and remove the one that was lodged in there pretty good," he said looking at all of his family members in their eyes. "Is there anything else I can answer for anyone?"

Everyone stayed silent until Uncle Jack who was standing next to the surgeon reached his hand out and thanked him for saving his nephew's life.

"Oh, it's all a part of my job sir, but you are very welcome," Dr. Gavin said turning around and then leaving Barry's hospital room.

A few weeks went by and Barry was slowly progressing to being let out of the hospital. Yvonne had taken over for Barry and from the small reports and updates he got from Jerry or

Harmony, she was handling her duties as President very well. In fact, Ursula and a few of the Cabinet members themselves thought she was doing an amazing job.

They pointed to a small incident that happened over in Benghazi. There was a bomb that went off at the US Embassy and as there was a lot of confusion in the beginning, Yvonne stayed cool, calm and collected. She asked the right questions, she was clear and concise with her directives.

Her small sample size of being the commander in chief, got Barry thinking. Should he really run for President or should he just take four years off?

For now, he decided that he needed to get rest. The more he slept, ate, and slept again, the more his body was going to respond and recover.

It had now been a month since he was shot and admitted into the hospital. Dr. Gavin kept to his promise and checked on Barry daily up until the night before he was going to be released.

"I got some good news for you Barry," Dr. Gavin called him by his first name because by now he and Barry had seen each other so much that Barry insisted that he call him by his first name. "You are cleared to leave, well, tomorrow morning, we want one more night with you to ensure that all the boxes are checked off, okay?"

"You and the entire team here at the hospital have done a fine job in helping me recover Doc," Barry said smiling from ear-to-ear.

"Just remember to take your meds, see your counselor and your physical therapist?" Dr. Gavin said with big eyes as if to say 'are you hearing me?'

Barry nodded in approval and the doctor shook his hand and walked out of the door.

By now, Barry's hospital room had a ton of plants, flowers, balloons, stuffed animals and he had a garbage bag full of 'get well cards' sitting over by the couch. Once a day, for the past week, he would stand up and sit over at the couch reading each of them.

The next morning, he slowly got up from his bed and made his way over to the couch that was next to the window overlooking downtown Pittsburgh. He dug in the bag and opened up a 'get well' card.

Some of the cards made him laugh and others made him shed a tear; for his tears were not because he was sad but because he was thankful. He was thankful to be alive and he was thankful that his life was exactly where it needed to be.

He was breathing; he had his mind in a solid state, he was set to be married in just a few months to a beautiful loving woman who was with him every-step-of-the-way during this issue.

Why rock the boat with all of this and run for another term? Why not think about taking time off and to focus on his marriage and perhaps having and raising children?

Financially, he was set; he had a lot of money in the bank and could afford to take four years; heck he had enough money to take 20 years off if he so chose to.

Barry sat there on the hospital couch, looking out into the Pittsburgh skyscrapers, he looked down at the hustle and bustle of the work world and was in deep thought.

He thought to himself: "Maybe this is it? Maybe this shot to the neck was a shot in the ass to think about my life and where it's at?"

Trina interrupted his thought process as she entered the room with a small suitcase of Barry's clothes for him to put on as today was the day he got to go back to the White House.

She put the suitcase down on the ground and saw an expression on his face that she had never seen before. It was a cross between confusion, fear and confidence all at the same time.

"Honey? What's the matter?" she asked Barry.

Barry didn't say a word. He was just about to talk to her and tell her something but instead he looked out onto the landscape outside and took a deep breath.

Made in the USA
San Bernardino, CA
31 October 2016